OBLIGATED

Lori Bell

This book is a work of fiction. Names, characters, places and incidents are the product of the author's imagination or are used fictitiously. Any resemblance to actual events, locales, or persons, living or dead, is coincidental.

Copyright © 2018 by Lori Bell

All rights reserved. This book or any portion thereof may not be reproduced or used in any manner whatsoever without the express written permission of the publisher except for the use of brief quotations in a book review.

Cover photograph by CanStock Photo

Printed by CreateSpace

ISBN 978 1984133755

DEDICATION

For those of you who have found your soul mate.
When our paths cross with that one person who gets us,
our lives are forever changed.

CHAPTER 1

The line was three people deep. Charli waited last. She glanced fleetingly around the coffeehouse. Social settings and people just weren't her thing anymore. Consequently, she looked down at the floor. Someone had dropped a shiny new penny. She didn't pick it up. She randomly noticed that the twenty-something guy in front of her wore classic black Converse on his feet. She was trying to distinguish if those shoes were high-tops, but the pant legs of his faded khakis hung too long. The line was moving quickly. One more person and she would be next to order. The coffeehouse was Charli's guilty pleasure. She didn't have many of those left in her life anymore. Okay, none. A vanilla latte was it.

She heard the man in Converse sneakers order an iced salted caramel mocha. The service was quick and friendly there. For Charli, courtesy and smiles were an added bonus, but timeliness was much more appreciated as she had to get home.

Converse guy stepped aside to grab a napkin and a straw, as Charli moved up to the counter and spoke the two glorious words to jumpstart her day. *Vanilla latte.*

Charli made her way up the stairway attached to the outside of the apartment building. The steps weren't rickety, but they were hardly the sturdiest. In bare feet, when she dared to in the summertime, Charli inevitably ended up with a splinter from the weathered wood. Today the air was chilly, but the sun was warm on her face. Her toned legs on her five-eight frame hustled her up the stairway in tight faded denim and worn brown faux leather boots that reached her calves. Careful to hold her latte in one hand, she pushed up the sleeves of the pale pink, chunky turtleneck sweater when she reached the closed door of her apartment. She turned the doorknob. *He had remembered to unlock it for her. Good, because she never brought a key with her.*

A lamp was lit near the end of the faded beige sofa, and the television was on in the living room, a little too loud for Charli's liking at a quarter after seven in the morning. The smell of burnt toast filled her nostrils as she closed the door behind her.

"Hey, good morning," Charli said to her husband of five years as he made his way from the kitchen to her, now standing in the middle of the living room. She noticed his sandy brown curly hair was still damp from the shower, and he needed a haircut again. The unruly curls were touching the back of the collar on his white dress shirt. He wore gray dress pants again today. Every other day those were his pick. His black loafers looked fairly new again. What a difference a little shoe polish could make.

"Good morning to you," Grayson Jade smiled, and kissed her quickly on the lips. He noticed the half-full plastic cup in her hands. "Again? That could be money saved, Charli."

She backed away from him, resisting the urge to roll her eyes. "I'll give up this when you kick the nicotine." He playfully swatted at her tight ass, and Charli muffled a giggle as she snuck away quickly and stepped into their small kitchen. There was a reason she worked all night long, to be home during the daytime hours. For that little blond-haired boy sitting at the kitchen table.

His facial expression didn't alter when he saw her, but his light blue eyes reacted. His arms flapped, hitting the tabletop twice, and he made an excited sound which was a cross between a wail and squeal. Liam was three years old now, and was labeled as developmentally delayed. He was thought to be nonverbal, there were some words though. He said, *mama, daddy, sleep, eat,* and *no*. Most of the time he relayed his wants and needs. But so many other times, Charli was left to read his mind. In a toddler's body, Charli's son wasn't an infant anymore, but in so many ways he still was. There was no official diagnosis for him. Not yet. Charli and her husband didn't have the funds or reliable insurance for additional blood work that could give them a definite label for a syndrome or a disorder. But what did it matter? Liam was healthy, physically. He just had many, many cognitive setbacks.

It was difficult to accept, but Charli was getting there. *What other choice did she have?* Grayson still had not entirely wrapped his mind around it. He held out hope for a *normal* toddler, a son like everyone else had. For Charli, that was false hope. Their difference of opinion —and level of acceptance— had caused a rift between the two of them. A rift they chose to ignore most of the time. Charli had embraced reality. This was her child, and she was going to love him and care for him as he was. Unrealistic expectations had already gotten her nowhere for too long.

"Hey buddy," she spoke warmly to her son as she kissed him on the top of his blond head and momentarily closed her eyes.

OBLIGATED

Jack prepared to take off his Converse sneakers when he entered the front door of the one level, ranch-style brick house. Careful not to spill his plastic cup now half full of mocha, he bent down to untie and slip out of his shoes. He could see the faint tire marks on the hardwood floor at his feet.

Married for three years to the love of his life, their life together already had not been what either of them imagined. "Jack, is that you?" His wife, Laney called out from somewhere in the house. He assumed she was in the kitchen.

"It's me," he answered, as he saw her rolling her wheelchair from around the far corner, through the kitchen doorway.

"Oh, I thought you were going to the office today?" she asked him, as Jack noticed she was dressed for the day. He had become accustomed to seeing her in stretchy yoga pants and t-shirts since she became confined to that chair. And her long dark brown hair was simply pulled back into a low ponytail.

"I am," he nodded. "I realized I forgot my laptop when I stopped for coffee."

"That's not coffee, it's more like melted candy," his wife teased him.

"Either way, my brain thinks I have to have it," he smiled, as he set the cup down on the sofa table and glanced around the living room for his laptop.

"You left it on the kitchen table."

"I did?" Jack started to walk en route to the kitchen, but Laney stopped him.

"My PT will be here in a few minutes, but I want to talk to you. Maybe over dinner tonight?" Laney suggested.

"Sure. I'll be home early," Jack said nothing more. He kissed the top of her head, then made his way to the kitchen to retrieve his laptop and left their house before his wife's physical therapist arrived.

Jack knew what the conversation topic would be during dinner, and right now he couldn't dwell on it anymore than he already had ever since a few days ago when he overheard his wife and her therapist talking. *I want to have a baby. My doctor says there's no medical reason why I can't.* When Jack heard the physical therapist's direct response, he caught himself holding his breath. *There are a few things you need to learn before you're ready to tackle taking care of another human being. Like acceptance. Accept what happened to you, and who you are now — imperfections and all. A baby will not make this world of yours perfect again.*

Jack stared out of his office window. It wasn't much of an office. Just empty space in a building adjacent to Brighton Street, which was basically a traditional *Main Street* in Savannah, Georgia. The zoning was a confusing nightmare down there. Apartment housing, office space, business complexes, and restaurants. He wasn't complaining too much though because the coffeehouse was within walking distance. *His guilty pleasure.* The desk he used consisted of a card table cluttered with magazines, sketch pads, and his laptop. And he had a decent stationary cushioned chair parked near it. Jack's company had yet to be launched. But one day, he would be the man behind his own label.

OBLIGATED

Jack Horton had drawing and design skills, along with talent and creativity. He lacked knowledge of the business and marketing aspects though, and he tried to make up for that by reading trade journals. His sketch pads were full, his digital storyboards that were logged on his laptop had totaled in the thousands now. Jack copyrighted enough sketches to get a decent start, to take the leap toward his dream to become a fashion designer. But he hadn't done anything more than accept the building space downtown Savannah, which his father-in-law had leased for him eighteen months ago. The Jack Horton he used to be had unparalleled perseverance. Being affected by tragedy slowed him down. Halted his plans. Guilt had seeped into his mind and heart, and made itself at home. *If I pursue this, it has to be with my wife by my side.* That was their plan before one accident altered everything.

Jack and Laney were an ideal pair. From the moment they met as seventh graders in a junior high English literature classroom, they knew it was love. Soul mates. Partners. They both had found their person. They were each other's first kiss — and first everything else. They discovered who they were as individuals and as partners. The more their lives intertwined, the happier it made them. When Jack felt the pull to be a designer, Laney dreamed of turning a sewing hobby into a career. They imagined Jack's designs on sketch paper coming to life in Laney's hands as she had the mechanical skills for sewing and cutting all types of fabric. It wasn't just about the fact that Jack could draw. In Laney, he recognized the talents he lacked to become a successful designer. She had an eye for color and texture, and the ability to visualize concepts in three dimensions. She understood and explained endlessly to him how fabrics move, drape, breathe and react when worn. Jack and Laney devoted hours of their lives to understanding fashion, learning from each other, and being inspired. Together, it was their dream.

And then one day all of their hopes and expectations were altered.

Six months after their graduation from Savannah College of Art and Design, they got married at The Cathedral of St. John the Baptist. The church was the skyline of Savannah, complete with two white and turquoise spires at the structure's highest point. While they stood in front of the altar, and everyone they loved, Jack told Laney that those conical, tapered points on the Cathedral symbolized how united they saw no limits and would reach new heights in their love and life together.

Just a mere few weeks later, Laney left their home in Whitemarsh Island to drive six miles to downtown Savannah. At Skidaway Road and Victory Drive was where most of Savannah came together from every corner of the city. The small intersection, which served as a main thoroughfare of the city, was heavily traveled. And highly at risk for collisions at those corners. In broad daylight, first thing in the morning, Laney never saw the vehicle coming to her left. She had the right of way, the traffic light ahead was green. She saw it clearly even though the sun was blinding as she pulled down her visor and still squinted behind sunglasses. Cars were flowing in her lane, and Laney's speed was forty-eight in a fifty-mile-an-hour zone. But then there was that vehicle coming at her left that never stopped at its red light. In the middle of that intersection at the heart of the city of Savannah, a truck twice the size of the car Laney was driving had plowed into her at a speed of sixty miles an hour on a road where speed limits were changeable at thirty, forty, and fifty miles an hour. The driver of the truck defied the red light. It could have been the blinding sun. Perhaps the driver was distracted. Whatever the case, it didn't matter after he hit Laney.

The abrasions, the broken bones, and the bruises eventually healed. It was Laney's spinal cord injury that effected and permanently damaged the thoracic nerves in the middle of her back. Laney was —after just an instant in time, a horrific split second— paraplegic. She had no use of the lower half of her body. Her legs would no longer carry her. At twenty-three years old, her means to move would forever be in a wheelchair.

Jack forced his eyes closed as he sat with his elbows on the card table at the window that spanned the entire front of the building he called his office, but still housed no store. He, again, was trying to force away that awful memory of his contradictory emotions—the moment he was beyond grateful his wife was going to live—she had survived that terrible accident—but knowing a part of her was lost forever. Laney would never be the same —or whole— again. *Could she survive that? Could they?* Three years later, together they were surviving but that was all.

Jack peered out the window for a moment as he saw a mini yellow school bus come to a stop cattycornered across the street. He watched a blond-haired little boy, who he would easily describe as a toddler, cling to a woman. He assumed she was the child's mother as they both had the same white-blond hair color. It was an obvious struggle for her to get him onto the bus. As she held the boy close to her body and climbed one step at a time, Jack could see little arms and legs flailing.

Had his store window or door been open, Jack may have heard crying or screaming. He watched this scene with interest. *Had a bus stopped there every day? It was considerably smaller than the average sized school bus.*

He wasn't sure why, but Jack continued to watch and wait as the bus sat idle for a quite a few minutes. The child must have eventually been secured in a seat, because finally the woman stepped off the bus, the door closed behind her, and the driver eased into the side street traffic and drove off.

The woman started to step off of the curb, and Jack stood up so fast from his chair partly underneath the card table that he bumped his upper legs on it and noisily shifted the lightweight table from its place. All the while, he never took his eyes off of what was going on outside. He heard brakes squeal and then saw a compact black car speed off. The woman had stepped off of the curb onto the cobblestone street. Whether she looked both ways or not, it happened too suddenly to tell before she fell backwards onto the grass above the curb. The driver of the car never stopped to see if she was okay. It wasn't a hit and run, but it damn near could have been.

Jack's heart was pulsing in his ears as he pushed open the glass front door, and ran as fast as his legs would allow. He reached the curb, just as the woman sat up and started to pointlessly use both of her hands to dust off the visible grass stains on her denim.

"Are you alright?" Jack called out to her, before he was too close, and invaded her personal space. He didn't want to startle her any more than she already had been.

Charli looked up, feeling more embarrassed than pained anywhere. "Um yes, just a little frazzled," she admitted, and Jack was close enough to see her eyes were blue.

"I should have gotten the license plate number, but the car sped away too fast," Jack stated, but he was most concerned that she was hurt. Vehicles crashing into things — and people — now scared the hell out of him. *If only Laney had also been unharmed on the roadside.*

"It's fine. As I said, I was already frazzled and didn't pay much attention when I stepped off the curb." Charli looked down at the road from where she was seated on the grass. This man in loose-fitting khaki pants was wearing Converse tennis shoes. *Had the man in the coffeehouse this morning also been wearing a red half-zip pullover? Were they one in the same?*

"Okay," Jack stated, not knowing what else to say. *Should he offer to help her up? Should he just go back across the street, or stay to be certain she was fine?* "I don't want to freak you out, I just thought you might need help."

Charli smiled and muffled a laugh. "You're not freaking me out. I do a pretty good job of freaking out on my own." She rolled her eyes at herself, and Jack chuckled.

"We all are capable of that one," Jack added, and without a second thought, he reached out his hand and offered it to her. If Charli hesitated, it was only for a mere second. She accepted his hand and help as she got to her feet. Nothing hurt. Just her pride. And she had momentarily forgotten how heart wrenched she felt after putting her son on the bus. It wasn't the first time. This was month two of his first year of early childhood education, which allowed three year olds to get the services they needed in a classroom setting very much like prekindergarten, but fit for children with special needs. *Special needs*. God those two words together still put Charli's mind and heart through turmoil.

"Thank you," Charli said, releasing her hand from this kind stranger who had come out of nowhere once she fell on her ass. She used both of her hands to dust off that ass right now, but she imagined it to be heavily grass-stained, as were her hands and parts of the front of her denim.

"You're welcome. Glad you're okay," Jack said, as he started to step off the curb.

"Where did you come from anyway?" Charli blurted out, realizing she had just stalled his attempt to leave and return to wherever.

"Oh, just across the street. See that corner building over there that looks abandoned — with no sign, no activity in or out? That's my store, or at least it will be a store someday." That was probably too much information from one stranger to another, but for Jack it was easy to admit his current career status was in progress. Jack watched her nod her head, as she knew the location he mentioned.

"What kind of store? I mean, what type of business are you opening?" Charli was curious, as it had been a long time since the For Rent sign was taken down on the old Subway building and there hadn't been much talk around the city regarding who leased it or what it was going to be once up and running.

"I'm a clothing designer," he spoke with less confidence in his tone than he once did. *You're way out of practice, Jack Horton.*

"Seriously?" Charli was intrigued. "So you have a label or something like that?"

Together, Jack and Laney had dreamed up hundreds of brand names, or tags, that they could have used. Jack wanted to share his initials with Laney, because this was going to be their team effort, their dream. But, Laney had insisted time and again that the designs were his alone. She just offered insight and tweaks from the background, and was sincerely all too happy to watch him shine. Laney wanted to wear his label one day, simply called JACK in all caps.

"JACK," Jack spoke, imagining the big, bold capital letters in his mind and wondering how cheesy he would sound to speak that detail. *In all caps.* "My name is Jack Horton, and my label will be JACK."

"I see," she smiled. "That's very exciting for Savannah, Georgia."

"Not really," he shrugged. *But maybe someday...*

It's more exciting than my life, Charli thought. And then her mind immediately centered on how the bus should have arrived at school by now. She wondered if Liam got off of it without a struggle. If she allowed herself, she could easily go crazy worrying about everything that took place in those three hours of school when her little boy was without her.

Jack noticed her sudden preoccupation. "So this is a school bus stop?" he brought up what he saw from the window earlier.

"Yes, my son goes to prekindergarten." It wasn't prekindergarten. It was early childhood education for very young children with special needs. Still, Charli was far from ready to share that information with just anyone. Or, no one.

"That's great," Jack offered. "I did see you put him on the bus. Cute kid."

"Thanks," Charli replied. "I should go."

"Of course, yeah, me too," Jack responded.

"Thanks again for checking on me, flat on the ground here," Charli smiled. "Good luck with your line, or label — Jack."

Jack nodded. *Luck, yeah.* He didn't need *luck*. He needed his wife to be the way she was before the accident robbed her of her legs — and cheated the both of them out of what felt like everything. Jack needed for *everything* to be the way it once was just as much as Laney did. But they both knew all too well this was reality. Limitations and a handicap consumed their life now. Absolutely nothing good had come from the day their lives changed forever. Nothing at all.

As Charli walked one way to her apartment complex, Jack walked in the opposite direction, back to his store.

CHAPTER 2

Charli was again headed up the stairway attached to the outside of the building that housed her apartment. She had less than three hours before Liam would be getting off of that bus she just struggled to put him on. She had been wearing the same clothes for nearly fifteen hours, all throughout her twelve-hour work shift and still this morning as she readied her son for school. Right now, Charli only wanted to strip herself of those clothes and linger in a hot shower. Sleep would have to wait.

She was climbing the stairs one floor below her apartment when her neighbor, Vera Faye, peeked her head from an open window. The chilly air appeared to have caught her breath before she spoke. "How'd it go this morning honey?" Vera was referring to Liam's transition at the bus stop. There really was no one else, in Charli's mind, who fully understood Liam's needs and her tribulations as his mother. Vera Faye was trained to understand. She was in her mid sixties and still working as a therapist. Her license was in both developmental and physical therapies. Vera was the one who initially detected Liam's delays as a baby. She was compassionate and gentle when she suggested to Charli that *something could be wrong*. That was a moment etched in Charli's mind. There was dull ache in the pit of her stomach. Her chest felt heavy. A part of her had wanted to deny it, to lash out, to threaten never to speak to her neighbor and friend again. But it was the other part of her — the fraction of her mind and her heart that already knew, already wondered and suspected — that wanted to take action. To help her son.

Charli stopped mid step and looked under the railing, level with Vera. Her short, curly hair was jet black, her large wire rimmed glasses perfectly matched. "Not much different than usual. He didn't want to go, I forced him, and now all I can think about is how he's doing."

"It'll get easier, honey." *Honey.* No one else used terms of endearment and meant them the way Vera did. Charli at least felt that way. This woman wasn't just a friend and neighbor. Vera Faye was like a mother to Charli, but more realistically old enough to be her grandmother. "Routine is gold to that boy, but it takes time to adjust and accept change. Look how far you've come in three years."

OBLIGATED

"I'm still learning and adjusting," Charli sighed, unwilling to entirely acknowledge the compliment, "but I've accepted the tiny baby boy that I brought home from the hospital swaddled in a blue blanket was extra special all along."

"And Grayson? Has he come around at all?" Charli emotionally wanted to shut down every time Vera insinuated that Grayson needed to *come around* or accept what was fact. Grayson was a man. A man who had a son. All men expect too much from their boys. It was a male thing. *We're tough. We're strong. We don't have time for bullshit. Snap out of it.* Grayson was all of those things, but he was also book smart. Charli rolled her eyes at the number of times she heard him say, *there has to be documentation out there somewhere on this. There's an answer, a solution.* There was no quick fix. There was no fix at all. Charli knew they were dealing with Autism. She didn't want to accept it at first either. She grieved for the son she thought she had given birth to. She would have sacrificed anything for him to be able to give her more than fleeting eye contact and randomly spoken words.

"He's Grayson. He'll read and research until the end of time," Charli smiled a little, and Vera nodded. She would drop the subject now. Charli obviously had not felt like talking about how she needed her husband's unwavering support and understanding. But she believed he was trying. And that's all that mattered.

Jack came home at a few minutes before five o'clock. His intentions were to help Laney prepare dinner, possibly even go to the grocery store for ingredients. When he pulled into the driveway, a minivan he had not recognized was already parked there. He just assumed a therapist drove a different vehicle than he was accustomed to seeing there.

After Jack closed the door behind him, he got out of his shoes. He never called out to Laney, expecting to hear her talking to the guest somewhere in their house. His thoughts were interrupted by the scent of something cooking, and it smelled amazingly good to him. He had not eaten anything all day, and that caramel mocha first thing this morning hardly held him over.

Jack followed the scent of what he hoped was dinner cooking in the kitchen. He turned to walk through the arched doorway, and first he just stared at Laney.

She placed a wine glass on the counter, level with her wheelchair. Her cheeks were a little flushed, which always used to happen when she drank her first glass of anything alcoholic. He watched her turn down a burner on the stove. Something delicious was simmering in that large skillet. *When was the last time Jack had seen her drink, and cook!* But that's not why he was staring. It was her hair. The lazy low ponytail, just pulled back to get it out of the way, was missing. Her long dark locks were down and hanging freely on her shoulders. Those shoulders were partly bare, as she wore what the designer in Jack knew was a cold shoulder dress. It was hunter green and it reached just above her knees. She wore heather grey suede booties on her feet. Her legs were bare. She had lost some of the muscle tone in her limbs, especially her once toned legs of an avid runner. Even still, she looked beautiful.

Laney turned her wheelchair and caught Jack's eye. He was staring. The change in her already sparked his attention. This evening had to go well. Laney needed for things to be okay between them again. Better than okay. And she was certain a baby, a chance to be a family with her husband, was the answer. Because she had nothing else left to give him. Nothing to contribute to a marriage that barely began before tragedy crushed her legs — and all of their hopes and dreams.

"You're here, and hungry I hope," Laney smiled, and for a fleeting moment Jack saw the woman he loved before the accident. The beauty in her eyes and on her face. The spark, the life in her, that had been gone for so long. *It could happen.* He saw past her limitations, that chair. And he knew the reason he felt that way so strongly right now was because Laney was finally allowing him to. If she accepted herself, she would be open to him loving all of her — her handicap and all. That was precisely it though. *Why? Why now had Laney wanted to change?* It was her quest to get pregnant. *And then what?* Jack thought. *What happens when she sinks back down into the throes of sorrow and grief and self pity? The baby, their baby would suffer.* Jack couldn't do it. He wouldn't bring a child into this world, into their unbalanced environment.

"Look at you. You're radiant, you're preparing a meal that smells amazing and yes I'm beyond starved." Jack walked toward his wife at the stove. This was what he — and her doctors and therapists— had been telling her. She can live and do so many of the things she used to, she only needed to improvise and be patient with herself and her surroundings.

Nothing was impossible. Jack was contradicting himself now, as he pushed the thought out of his mind. There was no easy way to prepare for the conversation his wife wanted to have with him tonight.

    Following dinner, they both claimed to have overeaten. Jack sat back in his chair and smiled. "That was so good, thank you," he said. It didn't matter if Laney had not prepared the meal. Her father's housekeeper, who also served him as a chef, had cooked and delivered it. All Laney had to do was heat it on the stovetop. Chicken Alfredo, topped with fresh mushrooms. It was a recipe neither of them had eaten before. It was new and different, especially after becoming so accustomed to take-out and quickly prepared food for one or the other, or shared between them.

    "It was good. I'll tell Alice you loved it," Laney smiled. She was still seated in her wheelchair, pushed up to the table. They hadn't kept all four chairs around their kitchen table in order to leave an open space for Laney to easily pull up her wheelchair. Her physical therapist had stressed the importance of strengthening her arms and upper body and how she needed to utilize those muscles regularly, for things like moving from her wheelchair to a dining chair at the table. Jack didn't push the issue, but he did recognize how Laney never made the effort to transition from her wheelchair unless she absolutely had to.

"So why did Alice leave her van here?" Jack asked, remembering the unfamiliar vehicle on their driveway when he came home.

"She didn't. She drives a black sedan," Laney answered. "The new, charcoal grey minivan complete with leather interior and special hand controls for acceleration and brake, is mine."

Jack furrowed his brow. He could almost see Laney holding her breath behind her smile. "Yours?"

"My father helped me today. I told him I was ready, it's time for me to get out there again. I want to be more independent." Again, Laney cautiously smiled, and waited for Jack to be happy about this.

"Your father helped you? Don't you mean he bought you a brand new vehicle? Dammit Laney, could we be any more indebted to that man!" Jack pushed his chair back so hard from the table that the chair legs screeched on the hardwood floor.

"Indebted? You know he's not keeping score," Laney never flinched or raised her voice as she watched her husband push his lower back up against the kitchen counter and fold his arms across his chest.

"I wish you would have talked this over with me first," Jack stated in a quieter tone of voice, in an effort to calm himself down.

"You don't think it's time?" Laney put him on the spot with that question. She knew how badly he wanted her to make the best of her limitations.

"Of course I do. I think anything you do to make your quality of life better and more enjoyable is progress," Jack stated. "I just need for you to see my side of this. Your father bought this house for us. I've never seen a monthly payment. The business I'm supposed to launch is housed in a building that your father leased for me. Our bank account replenishes itself with deposits, I don't know how often, and you and I are both jobless. We are adults, riding on the coattails of your wealthy father." The man owned banks all over the country, but two of the largest were located in Savannah, Georgia, and in West Palm Beach, Florida where his roots were.

"He doesn't look at it that way. You know that, Jack," Laney was not going to back down. She thought nothing of living off her father's wealth, especially since she viewed herself as an invalid. Standing beside her hospital bed following the devastation from the accident, Laney's father vowed through sobs to *always take care of her.*

"But I do," he replied.

"Get your label up and running," Laney abruptly suggested, and Jack was taken aback. "Do it. It's time you find the success you deserve."

"My intention was to pay your father back every penny," Jack spoke firmly, but he felt defeated. "It's getting way too out of hand for that now."

"I mean it, Jack. Show the world your designs," Laney was pushing him, and he didn't understand why. They didn't force any issue, or attempt to encourage each other anymore. When Jack first tried to be Laney's greatest cheerleader in the months following the accident, she only withdrew further from him — and the world around her.

"My designs? They were ours. It's been three years since you've even looked at anything I've sketched. It's not the same anymore. I can't do what I do without you. I've told you that from the beginning." This was the most honest Jack had been with his wife in a very long time. And perhaps this also was the most truthful he had been with himself. He was not going to take JACK the label anywhere — not without Laney.

"Let's make some changes in our lives," Laney spoke confidently. Her dark brown eyes were intense. "Let's start a family. I need a reason to get up in the morning, to love life again."

"We were talking about the label, not a baby," Jack held firm.

"More than one change will do us some good," Laney stated.

"I used to see JACK as our baby, and look what we both did to it. We gave up. We weren't courageous enough to pull together for a clothing line. How will we ever make it as parents?" Jack knew his words were harsh, but he was adamant about not bringing a child into this world. *What it if was too much for her to carry a baby to term? Or, what if she were to give up on the tiny, helpless human once it's born?* Jack didn't have it in him to raise a baby alone, nor to one day have to explain how his or her mother just gave up. He already watched his wife all but give up on life every single day since the accident paralyzed her.

"It takes time to build courage after something strikes you down," Laney defended herself, and them.

"Take a look at my designs. There are hundreds of them since—" Jack paused. There was no need to say it. He wasn't entirely sure that he was *good enough* anymore. He needed her in order to believe in himself — and the line.

"Make a baby with me," Laney tried not to sound like she was desperate.

I can't, Jack wanted to say to his wife, but he didn't know how to further explain his answer to her. So instead, he walked out — after saying he needed some time to think.

Charli was spent. She had not slept in well over twenty-four hours. A note in Liam's backpack informed her of his extremely difficult morning in school, and because he kept dwelling on everything that had happened there, his afternoon at home was challenging. He lashed out at Charli. He cried. He laughed. He smiled. He scowled. He was an emotional wreck. Charli tried talking to him. She explained that whatever happened in school many hours ago was over. She reminded her little boy that he was home now, and should try really hard to focus on his toys and the things that make him feel happy. Liam's face was blank as Charli spoke, and then the meltdown resumed. By the time Grayson came home from work, Charli was completely overwhelmed.

"You okay?" *Did he even have to ask?* He could hear their son banging his head against the wall in his bedroom. There was a preferred spot on the floor, in a far corner, where Grayson was sure Liam would one day split his head open from the repetitive blunt force.

"I need a minute," Charli said, as she attempted to step outside of their apartment.

"What? You're leaving? I just got home. What about dinner?" Grayson pressed her.

"I don't have a plan for dinner. I've had our son to deal with all afternoon. It's been a day, Gray." Charli all but held back the tears fighting behind her eyes.

"And I worked all day!" Grayson immediately raised his voice as if that was going to change anything. His wife needed a break, but he didn't want to deal with the head banger in the other room.

Charli glared at him. If she could have spoken without the overwhelming lump in her throat, she would have said, *fuck you*, before she walked out and slammed the door behind her.

She needed a minute.

CHAPTER 3

It wasn't so much that he wanted the coffee, his stomach was still satisfied from dinner. He just sought out the atmosphere of the coffeehouse. Music was playing low, the window seat allowed him to watch the activity on the street, as well as the sunset. Jack could see his store, the unmarked and empty place, from where he stared directly out of the window. It represented nothing to him. Given to him by his overzealous father-in-law. Not earned. Not in the least.

And now Laney wanted him to just snap his fingers and make himself successful? And get her pregnant, too. Jack thought about how long it had been since he touched his wife, and when she had actually responded to him. Too long. It scared him now. *Would he hurt her? Would she feel him like before?* They had so much to talk about, and here he was alone at the coffeehouse. He had walked out on her.

OBLIGATED

The door chimed and Jack watched a woman walk in. She looked as forlorn as he felt. For a second, Jack thought he recognized her. Blonde hair, piercing blue eyes. And then he remembered. She was the woman at the bus stop who he saw almost be struck by a car. Well according to her, it wasn't a near miss, but what Jack had witnessed was alarming enough for him to run across the street to her rescue.

Jack watched her body language as she got in line to order. *You just never know what other people are going through.* Jack was well aware of hardship. A part of him wanted to know other people's stories just so he wouldn't feel as alone in his own struggle.

As Charli turned away from the counter with her coffee in hand, she intended to look for an open seat, preferably by the window, but instead she made direct eye contact with Jack. Dark hair, dark eyes. She immediately recognized him. *Converse guy. Side of the road rescue man.* Charli waved. To be polite she stepped in his direction.

"Hi," Jack said first.

"Jack, right?" She remembered him and his label.

He didn't know her name. Her eyes seemed sad to him still. Or possibly just tired. Jack nodded. "Forgive me, but I never asked your name earlier."

"Charli with an I," she smiled a little as she spoke.

"Catchy," Jack responded. "That would make a much better label than JACK in all caps."

Charli laughed and then sipped her coffee, which she ordered straight and black this time. Her stomach was too empty for anything overly sweet. "Is everything okay in your world?" He wasn't sure what made him ask. Maybe her sad blue eyes. Perhaps he felt connected to her because everything was not wonderful in his world.

"Can 'okay' truly be defined? If so, I don't believe any of us could nail it. We've all got something weighing on us." Charli all but shrugged as she spoke, and suddenly Jack wished he could handle his problems so positively and with such grace.

"What's your something?" Jack asked, sort of surprising himself. He needed to dismiss the small talk and get home. But this seemed like more than chit chat or filler. Charli looked like she needed a friend. And Jack felt the same.

Charli hesitated, and then thought *why not?* "You saw me put my *something* on the special needs bus this morning." There it was. She said those two words together as if it wasn't the end of the world. For most people, that would be a conversation ender. But not for Jack Horton. He also, for three years now, had been forced into being a part of the handicap world.

Charli set her coffee down on the high table where Jack was seated. She pulled out the chair across from him. This wasn't something she talked about at the top of her voice, or standing up in a public place. This was private, so she closed the space between her and Jack before she attempted to speak again. Then Jack beat her to it. "I don't want to pry, but what is your son burdened with?" Jack wondered if the toddler could walk as his memory flashed to Charli carrying him onto the bus.

He did recall his arms and legs flailing, so he assumed being mobile wasn't an issue. Laney was on his mind, that's all. To him, handicap meant not having use of your legs.

"I brought it up, so technically you're not prying," Charli smirked. "Liam, my three-year-old son, does not have a diagnosis. I'm told he's quirky and has developmental delays, but the doctors would like for him to have some genetic testing done to pinpoint a syndrome to match his behavior. I've done enough research of my own to know that my son, sooner or later, will be labeled with having Autism." Each time she spoke that word, she cringed. It just didn't come easy.

Jack watched her trace her finger on the rim of her coffee cup. "I'm sorry," he stated first. "I don't know much about Autism, but I recognize the pain on your face. Life just isn't easy for any of us, is it?" Charli wondered what plagued him. *Was it merely his quest to be a clothing designer?* Funny how he wanted a label and that was the absolute last thing Charli would ever seek — for her son.

When Charli stayed silent, Jack spoke again. "For your sake, I hope you're not juggling parenting your boy alone." He saw the ring on her finger. "Married?"

Charli spotted the plain gold wedding band on his hand as well. "Yes, fortunately. I actually ran out tonight when my husband came home from work. I couldn't take it anymore. The wailing, the head banging, the reactions my son has to the world around him. He's unable him to adjust to most things out of routine, or any change at all. School was really rough for him today," Charli sighed. "I just can't fix things for him sometimes. I felt defeated, I said I needed a minute. It's been more than a minute…"

Jack thought of doing the very same thing to Laney after dinner. He guessed he wasn't the only *jerk* tonight. Not that he believed Charli to be selfish or unkind. Everyone had a breaking point. "I understand," he told her, "more than you know." He paused for a moment. Talking to her was already making him feel less pity for himself, or at the very least not so alone. He knew Charli was staring and waiting for him to continue. "I know what it's like to live differently than the rest of the world, or so it feels that way. It's isolating, and unfair." Charli, however, had suddenly opened his eyes to the mere fact that there were others out there who understood. Charli was scathed too. She didn't think of her son as a burden any more than Jack believed that of his wife, but even so everyone's individual pain hurt like hell. And it was healthy to admit that.

Charli nodded her head. She wished Grayson could see the clarity that Jack obviously had about life, and its hardships. The problem with Grayson was he still looked for that quick fix, a cure all. The answer had to be in a book, or online somewhere. Jack appeared to be better in touch with his emotions. Again, Charli wondered why. *What had happened to make him get it?*

"I met my wife when we were in the seventh grade," he began, and Charli sat up in her chair, closer to the table. She wrapped both of her hands around her coffee cup and listened. "We were inseparable forever — all through junior high, high school, and we graduated from college with big dreams to work together on our label. I can't design to my full potential without her. We were married for only a few weeks… and there was an accident." Jack didn't tell this story often. *Actually, never. It was just too difficult.* "Someone's carelessness cost my wife the use of her legs. She was in a car accident here in downtown Savannah when some son of bitch ran a red light. She'll never walk again. And I've had to pretend that seeing her day after day confined to a wheelchair doesn't affect me in the worst way."

Charli covered her mouth with her hand. That's when she realized it was trembling. *My God, there was such pain in his world.* While their two situations were entirely different, Jack understood. The connection Charli felt to this man right now, right at this very moment, was as overwhelming as it was comforting. The two of them had crossed paths for a reason. Charli was certain of it, and Jack felt it too.

"You're trembling," he pointed out to her, as if she wasn't aware.

"I know," she responded. "I'm just so taken in by your story. I want to express to you how terribly sorry I am. How I feel for your wife, even though I do not even know her." *And how she had never been able to connect to anyone like this, over her private pain.* Not even Vera. It was because Jack had been there and understood what it truly was like to live a *different* life. They were people who felt helpless and determined to persevere, both at the same time.

"And I feel for you…your son…and your husband. I can't imagine the uncertainty that you have for your child's future," Jack stated, sincerely. "Talking to you has opened my eyes a little," he admitted. "My wife needs me, just as your son needs you. We are obligated to be there for them, but it's not out of duty or responsibility — it's for love."

The two of them stared at each other for a long moment. She only had a few sips of coffee, but Charli felt intoxicated. Words had brought her to that high point. This man was like an angel sent to her at the precise time.

"I think we should both go home and hold tight to who we love," Charli heard this man across the table from her say. She immediately nodded her head in complete agreement. She was so grateful for this stranger's guidance tonight. His hardship had put hers into full perspective. *She was not alone. She was stronger than she believed herself to be. My God, she was healthy and had full capacity of her limbs. She was put here on this earth to care for her son, to give him whatever it was that he needed from her.*

Charli felt the tears welling up behind her eyes. "Thank you," she said to him, as they both stood up simultaneously and walked together out of the coffeehouse before they parted ways.

CHAPTER 4

Charli made it home within minutes from the coffeehouse, which was located just two blocks, cattycornered from her apartment building. She had walked the cobblestones streets to get there earlier.

She climbed the outside stairway swiftly, but carefully as the night sky was already completely dark with the exception of the quarter moon. There was light coming from Vera's apartment, and more shown from her own, one level higher. When she reached the door, it was unlocked again.

As Charli stepped into the living room, she immediately saw Grayson and Liam. They were lying on the sofa pushed up against the wall to the right of her. Grayson had Liam wrapped tightly in the powder blue fleece blanket that was his favorite. Charli sighed to herself at the sight of them. *Those were her boys.* Grayson had come through for her. He gave their son what he needed — when she couldn't. *Why hadn't she thought of the blanket?* Charli had run out of ways to soothe him. And to calm herself as well.

Liam never took his eyes off of the television that was airing an old black and white movie. It didn't matter the show or movie, if it was black and white Liam was taken in every time. Grayson, however, was looking at her. Charli noticed he was still wearing his gray dress pants, with no socks and no shirt. He was hot-blooded, so to be able to hold someone in his arms, wrapped in a warm blanket, was sure to make him sweat. Grayson didn't appear uncomfortable as Charli sat down on the sofa at his feet. Again, Liam never looked away from the television. What Charli would not give for her little boy to come running to her when she walked through the door. Or, at the very least, make eye contact, or smile.

Charli began to go there again, to that hole of self pity. The what if's, the why me's. She thought of Jack and what he was going home to tonight — a wife whose healthy body had physically changed to crippled in an awful instant.

"Where were you?" Grayson's words interrupted her thoughts.

"The coffeehouse," she answered. "I'm sorry, I should not have run out like that. I was just…overwhelmed." Charli felt guilty for leaving, and ashamed for not being the one to calm Liam the way his father obviously had. Grayson moved off of the sofa and placed Liam in the same spot where he had been laying down. He re-tucked the blanket securely around him. Charli stood up, and bent forward to kiss her son on the top of his head. Again, no response. He had just stretched his neck around her to be in direct view of the television. She had been in his way. Charli followed Grayson into the kitchen.

Those sandy brown curls were matted on his head from lying down. He was shirtless, his stomach muscles were impeccably toned for a man who didn't regularly work out. She watched him pace barefoot on the hardwood floor. "Are you hungry?" Charli asked her husband, without noticing there was a used skillet on the stovetop.

"No, we ate grilled cheese," Grayson replied, expressionless, yet still evidently angry.

"I wasn't gone that long, was I?" she asked, implying that he could have waited for her to eat dinner.

"You walked out. I had no idea what time you were coming back," Grayson stated. "Liam was hungry. I knew he would eat a grilled cheese, so I did too." Charli was aware there wasn't much else in the house, no real amount of groceries to make a decent meal. It was still another week yet before she would get paid, and Grayson's paycheck had to cover the bills for water and utilities for the month. Her job as a hotel front desk clerk didn't keep them afloat, but it helped. The twelve-hour shifts, four nights a week, kept them from having to hire daytime care for Liam. They were in a financial slump. Grayson hadn't seen a raise since Liam was born. He enjoyed being a loan officer at a local bank, in Savannah, but Charli wished he would either make a point to move up the career ladder there, or find a better-paying job elsewhere. But that was a sore subject between them. Money and their son's issues were serious thorns in their marriage. They never could see eye to eye on either. Many times, since she got married, Charli had regretted not going to college to earn a degree and establish a career of her own.

Charli initially stayed silent, but then opted to defend herself. "I'm exhausted. I left Liam with you because I needed a break. I trusted that you would take care of him, and you did. Can we just leave it at that?"

Grayson nodded. "I can put him to bed when he's ready. He's had a bath. Water was something I tried as an attempt to calm him down, but it didn't work so the bath was quick."

"I noticed his wet hair when I kissed him," Charli smiled. "Thanks Gray. I owe you one." *But did she?* This was a partnership. Liam was *their* son. Give and take, picking up each other's slack should not be about evening the score.

He winked at her as she left the kitchen. All she wanted to do was take a shower and sleep. But instead, she walked back into the living room and sat down at her son's little bare feet, which had already found their way out of the bottom of the blanket. His tiny eyelids were closed now, so she stood again, carefully picked him up into her arms, and carried him down the hallway to his bed. *Another day survived.*

OBLIGATED

※

Jack parked on the driveway next to Laney's new minivan. He would offer to take practice drives with her, starting tomorrow, to help her feel more confident about being behind the wheel again. He tried to put himself in his wife's place so often. Now he was thinking about what it would be like to only use his hands to accelerate and stop a vehicle. His brain was trained to use his right foot to control the vehicle's movement. How does a person go from natural instinct to learning how to do everything all over again, in an entirely new way? There was such a fine line between being compassionate and being overbearing. Jack sometimes didn't know what Laney expected or wanted from him anymore, so he had done nothing.

The house was dark as he approached the front door, and used his key to unlock it before he stepped inside. He could hear the television on in their back bedroom, and there was light shining into the hallway. Jack slipped off his Converse and walked in socks down the hall. He looked at his feet, and he thought of the times during the days and weeks when they were first married and the two of them would race down that hallway, sliding in their socks, laughing, touching, kissing, and in a hurry to make it to the bedroom. It had been so long, too long, since Jack allowed himself to go there. To remember what it was like to be with her, to hold her. She shut down and pushed him away time and again, and inevitably Jack allowed her to.

He reached the open doorway, and saw Laney in their bed. The lamp was lit on the nightstand near her. The television was too loud for someone attempting to sleep, but Laney always could fall asleep anywhere and stay asleep through noise. Jack smiled to himself. For a moment, she looked whole again, as he watched her lying there. No wheelchair to be confined to. Just the beautiful girl he fell in love with from the second he saw her. She looked peaceful, and Jack at first thought he would leave her be. She was resting. It annoyed him though. It wasn't even seven o'clock in the evening and she again wanted to give up on the day at an early hour. He remembered a time when he had researched online signs for depression. He wondered then if Laney's need to sleep the days and nights away was a red flag for something serious. He left it at that, never speaking of it to her or to her doctors or therapists. *It is what it is.* Jack was done with that mindset now. He wanted a life with this woman, his wife. And she was going to have to meet him halfway.

He turned the television off, and walked over to her side of the bed. "Laney…" he spoke her name aloud, but she never stirred in her sleep. He moved closer and reached for her leg. He caught himself immediately. She wouldn't feel that touch even if she were awake. He swallowed hard the lump in his throat. *How fucking unfair.*

He moved onto the bed and sat alongside of her torso. She was flat on her back, still with closed eyes. He touched her bare arm. Laney always slept in a v-neck white t-shirt with a small pocket over the left breast, and only panties on her lower body. It didn't matter the season, that was her sleep attire. "Laney, babe, wake up." This time her eyes opened.

"You're home," she said to him, remaining still on her back, as he was seated close beside her.

"I just went for coffee," he admitted.

"I knew you wouldn't go far, or be gone long," she smiled. Laney was absolutely the most loving and forgiving person Jack had ever known. She never held a grudge toward anyone. Her greatest fault now was self pity. And it was slowly destroying her spirit. Laney had changed in ways Jack never believed were possible. She was withdrawn and angry, and most of that anger was geared toward the circumstances — and herself. But tonight, Jack got a glimpse of the old Laney again. She resurfaced. She was back, not completely, but close.

"Will you stay awake with me for awhile?" he asked her. "To talk."

She shook her head in disagreement first, and then spoke. "We can talk tomorrow. It's time Jack. It's time that we're close again. I still feel like a woman…down there." She wanted to tell him that she's not going to break. He can take her, ravish her, make love to her again. But she stopped talking when she saw the tears welling up in his eyes.

"I love you so much, Lane. But I'm afraid." She watched the tears spill over onto his cheeks and she reached up to wipe them with her fingers. Laney knew Jack's heart broke for her.

"I'm afraid too," she told him, "of losing you."

"Is that why you want a baby?" Jack didn't hesitate to ask her outright, first and foremost. *Before he allowed his body to respond to her completely.* He was already coming alive in places that he had forced himself to ignore for far too long.

"To trap you? To keep you in this marriage? No." Laney told him. "To feel as if I have a purpose again? Yes. I want to be a mommy. I want to give you a child. I want someone else to focus on besides my limitations. I need that so badly. Please, Jack."

He took her hand from his face, and he kissed her fingers. She lingered her fingers on his lips. She traced them, full and pink, and then she touched the end-of-the-day scruff on his chin. At this point, Jack was not going to ask her anything more. He wondered if she was at the stage in her cycle where she could definitely get pregnant. He worried he would regret doing this without asking her that significant question, but then he took one long, drawn out look into his wife's eyes and nothing else mattered but the two of them — and this moment.

She reached for him first. She used her arms and upper body strength to help him out of his red half-zip. She ran her palms over his bare chest, and she watched him close his eyes. She reached for the fly of his khaki pants and felt him hard and pushing to be free. He stood up beside the bed, and rushed to drop his pants and underwear to the floor. Laney reached for his manhood as it sprung to life. Jack again closed his eyes.

Before he climbed back onto the bed, he pulled off the sheet and duvet covering her body. She was wearing lacy pink panties. As he joined her in bed again, Jack watched her take the hem of her white v-neck t-shirt and move it up and off of her chest. Her breasts were bare, and not as full as he remembered them to be. He touched eagerly with his fingers first, and then pressed his lips to her. She was arching her upper body for him, as her lower half lay lifeless. He moved first to meet his lips with hers, and then and they kissed with force and passion.

OBLIGATED

Time stood still for them and they hungrily touched as if they were brand new to each other.

When Jack moved his hand to take off her panties, Laney joined her own hand over top his. "I can feel you there, Jack. Just spread my legs for me, please."

Jack's eyes widened. He did as she asked. He met his mouth with her core, and he didn't stop until she felt like a woman again. Laney was still panting when he entered her with care and an overwhelming sexual desire. With each thrust, she begged him to do what he needed to do to climax inside of her, *harder, faster,* and so he went there. He pushed his way through those thoughts of uncertainty. Making love to his wife was not the same, and it never would be again. *She would never wrap her legs around him. They couldn't get wild and change positions.* But he could do this for her. He wanted to feel like a man again. He desperately needed to free himself of all the pent up emotion. And finally. Finally. Jack closed his eyes with his release — as he thought of the blonde haired, blue-eyed *Charli with an I.*

CHAPTER 5

Liam had the giggles as he and Charli were walking down the outside staircase near their apartment. Charli was walking backwards, one careful step at a time, as she held his little hand in hers. She laughed with him, but stopped herself as she reminded him to be careful. Liam was still unsteady on his feet at times, and could be a bit clumsy as he mostly balanced on his toes. It was a sensory processing issue, and the doctors and therapists had told her that he may outgrow it. When they reached the bottom of the stairs, Liam had the hiccups from all of the laughing. His little pale face reddened with every hiccup. Charli smiled as she shook her head at her boy. *What a little handful. Such a joy at times. If only he could see the world as a less threatening place to be.* Nonetheless, Liam was having a good morning, and if Charli could have she would order thousands more of those easy starts to every day for her little boy.

OBLIGATED

Even the transition onto the bus was effortless. Charli stood on the curb for a moment, just watching as the bus pulled away. Already, in three years time, such a tiny human had taught her to be grateful for the little things.

The roar of the bus engine forced his gaze out of the window and onto the street. Jack saw her standing there. He hoped Charli's son was having a better day today. He recalled her saying how it was common for him to fluctuate between good and bad days. Just like everyone else, really, only with enhanced emotions. Their conversation at the coffeehouse the night before had been incredibly unexpected, but nice. It was simply *nice* to know someone else understood. Jack had gone home to Laney, not expecting what happened between them at all. His wife was on her way back to him. Just this morning, she was in better spirits and acting ready to tackle a brand new day. Her father was going out to practice driving with her. Jack had wanted to, but he kept quiet when Laney told him of her plans. She kissed him goodbye before work while she was soaking in a bubble bath. She assured Jack that the chairlift in the custom-made Jacuzzi would make it easy for her to help herself when she was ready to get out. It was another feature her father had funded to be added to their handicap-equipped home, but Laney was never willing to use it without the help of a therapist, or Jack. He smiled and truly felt grateful for this huge change for the better in their life.

Laney was his prime focus, but his designs also needed to be front and center in his mind if he was going to make anything of himself. It was either put the designs out there, or get a real job. It was time, Jack knew. He brought up the images on his laptop. His top one hundred. Those were the designs he was going to start with. Out of those, he would choose a gotta-have-it piece. He had seen other successful designers make their break with that one must-have. The wrap dress. The capri pants. The denim unisex shirt. And the list went on.

Jack's designs were developed and ready for show. He still believed he needed Laney's eyes on each piece before he attempted a prototype as an early sample, built and used as a test. He would ask her again tonight. But if she refused, this time Jack was going full speed ahead without her. *Now or never, JACK.*

There was a factory, based in New York, where Jack had made a few connections in college. He was still counting on their help to get his chance in the business. Those start-up funds would have to come from his father-in-law, and Jack was going to tuck his pride somewhere deep inside of him and take advantage of the financial help. He still imagined being successful enough one day to gradually pay back all he owed that man. *Wishful thinking.*

Jack was scrolling through his designs on the laptop screen, one by one, and tagging those he thought to have potential for his top one hundred. His focus was so deep that he never heard the first knock on the picture window of his store. A second tap caught his attention. He looked up and saw Charli staring at him through the glass. He raised his hand to wave. She waved back with a lopsided grin, as Jack stood up to go to the door.

"I didn't mean to interrupt," Charli said before Jack completely opened and then held the door for her. "You looked busy. I'm just headed for coffee, and I peeked in your window as I walked by." *Oh the number of times she had walked by that empty store. Funny how strangers come to know each other.*

"You're not an interruption, not at all," Jack spoke as she stepped inside of the almost completely vacant space.

"So this is it. The place where you'll plant the seed for success…"

Jack smiled at her words. "Maybe? I'm ready, I've been ready. The timing just wasn't right."

Charli nodded. "How are things at home, since last night?" It wasn't prying to ask him that question. Neither felt as though it was, because they had connected on a deep personal level the night before at the coffeehouse when both of them admitted to feeling defeated with the circumstances in their lives.

Jack thought of making love to Laney for the first time since the accident. His body had responded to her. He was starved for the physical attention. But his mind had been at war with uncertainty. And then he thought of Charli. It was wrong, and he was ashamed afterward. The very last thing he would ever do was be unfaithful to his wife. She was Laney. *The only woman he had ever touched. Ever truly loved. And that would always be a fact for him until the end of time.* Jack was that kind of man. Still, there was guilt. Guilt he could never admit to Charli. Yet, here she was, asking him about last night with his wife.

"Better," Jack answered. "She seems to be turning a corner in her recovery, with acceptance. Therapists and doctors have told us how important it is for people to learn to accept what happened to them, accept the change, before they can ever adjust to being someone different than they used to be. Laney has never been this close to showing an interest in reaching that point. I'm really proud of her."

Charli smiled. "That's wonderful. So, what do you think has finally put her there? Is it the idea of launching the label with you?" Charli was intrigued with her assumption, and Jack wondered if he should just go with that notion. It certainly would be easier than telling his newfound friend the truth.

"Not yet, but I hope she'll come around to the idea of helping me again," Jack admitted, first. He really did not have a lot of friends or family to confide in anymore. Since the accident, he had lost touch with so many of those who were once important, and front and center in his life. Tragedy tended to either bring people closer, or frighten them away. "I can't believe I'm going to tell you this," Jack stated as a matter of fact, as Charli watched him run his fingers through his short dark hair. She saw the gold wedding band on his finger again. "Laney wants to have a baby. She needs a purpose, and she wants that purpose to be a family for us."

"That's amazing," Charli reacted. "There's nothing, absolutely nothing, like bringing a child of your own into this world." Charli paused and thought of all the hopes and dreams she once had for her baby. Life certainly had a way of slipping in surprises and challenges. How many times hadn't she told herself what Vera had preached to her from the very beginning of her struggles with Liam? *Alter your expectations to make happiness and contentment exist in your lives.*

"I have my reservations," Jack spoke honestly as he stood facing Charli, in the middle of his empty store. She was tall, maybe five-eight to his six-foot frame. He was wearing his flat-soled Converse again, and he noticed now that she was in calf-high boots with a just-above-the-knees sweater dress. *Black dress. Brown boots. Long blonde hair. Piercing blue eyes.*

"Physically, can her body endure a pregnancy?" Charli asked, and then she was quick to add, "Please stop me if I'm asking something that makes you uncomfortable!"

"It's fine. I'd like to think we're friends, fast friends maybe," Jack laughed, "and friends are permitted to ask those kind of questions. It's a way to get to the heart of matter, isn't it?" Charli nodded with a sincere smile, as Jack continued. "The doctors have told her she's young and healthy and very capable of carrying a baby to full term. The baby would have to be taken by cesarean section, but many women must have or opt for that procedure anyway. For me, I'm more concerned what happens once the baby is born. Can my wife take care of an infant? Will she say she wants to and then sink into some sort of pity hole again? Don't misunderstand me, no one feels more heart-wrenching sympathy for Laney than I do. To be told you will no longer walk for the rest of your life, basically when your life was just beginning, was beyond unfair. But, I've lived every second of that life of limitations with her, and it's been so suffocating to watch my wife give up on everything. And now suddenly she tells me she has this new lease on life. And a baby is the answer. But is it?" Jack stopped talking. He felt both nervous and so at ease with Charlie. It was strange to explain. *He shouldn't be talking to another woman about his wife and his innermost feelings, should he?* But this was Charli. It was silly to think they were already connected somehow. If Jack believed in former lives, he would be certain beyond a reasonable doubt that their souls crossed paths before, in some other dynasty.

"I can't answer that for you," Charli began, "but I can tell you that we only get one life." How ironic that she had just said that when Jack was ridiculously imagining otherwise. "After Liam was born and his troubles surfaced, a wise, beautiful woman in my life told me that sometimes we have to alter our expectations to make happiness and contentment exist in our lives. If you have a baby with your wife, you'll raise that tiny human the very best way you know how. Will life be perfect? That's a big fat no. But, as you and I both have come to know well, whose is?"

Jack nodded his head repeatedly in unison with Charli's every word. She was some sort of angel sent to him at the most perfect time.

Charli believed the very same of Jack. They were most definitely a godsend to each other.

OBLIGATED

Their visit was abruptly cut short when Jack's cell phone rang and he checked the caller identification and regretfully told Charli he had to take the call. She left feeling reenergized regardless. It was Jack who later wished he would've had time to ask Charli how things were going at home. They had only spoken about him.

Charli grabbed a vanilla latte to-go across the street and hustled home to get a few pertinent things done before Liam returned from his few hours of school. She had to work at the hotel again all night, so making a plan for dinner and giving the apartment a quick clean had to happen this morning.

She was now barefoot and still wearing her sweater dress while vacuuming the living room carpet when she turned with a start to find Grayson attempting to make his way into the apartment without alarming her. She obviously never heard him if he had tried to talk over the noise.

"Oh my word! Gray! You scared the hell out of me!" Charli had shut off the vacuum in a flustered instant, and Grayson stood in the middle of the room with both of his hands up, a signal for mercy she assumed.

"Sorry! I forgot my cell this morning. I'll be in and out in a flash." *Did anyone ever say 'in a flash' anymore?* Charli couldn't help but smile. His throwbacks oftentimes amused her. He wore black pants today with a powder blue shirt and a tie that had too many primary colors and not a single one matched. *Whatever, it works for me,* Grayson would say if Charli had pointed that out to him.

Sometimes a moment like this was nice. She was alone with her husband, without their child's anxiety forcing them to feel on edge, or be proactive, responsible parents. Charli told herself she needed to appreciate those moments more. Sure it was just a forgotten cell phone and a quick return home, but she suddenly saw it as something more.

"Why are you looking at me like that?" Grayson grinned. He thought she looked exceptionally sexy, barefoot in a dress right now.

"Like what?" she teased him. "Like we might wanna lock the door?"

Grayson's eyes widened. The mere thought of his wife's proposal immediately turned him on to the idea. "We never lock the door..." he stated, while walking backwards to that very door and turning the deadbolt as Charli giggled.

On the floor in the short carpeted hallway leading back to their bedroom already laid a partially knotted ugly tie, a mangled sweater dress, and a rumpled pair of black dress pants.

On their queen-size bed, Grayson quickly removed the rest of his clothing while straddling his wife in her matching black bra and panties.

He kissed her hard, starved for more of her. And Charli responded to him with an eagerness he hadn't felt from her in a very long time. She reached for him, and stroked him until he groaned, "You're killing me." Charli smiled at his words. Grayson tore off her bra and buried his face into her breasts. She arched her back and he slipped an eager hand into her panties.

OBLIGATED

Two of his prominent fingers found her core. Charli closed her eyes. And begged him not to stop. "More. Please. Touch me, Gray." She panted, she called out his name over and over, not caring if the barriers were paper thin in that aged apartment building. When she abruptly went limp, spent from her release, Grayson rolled her body over and guided his wife to her knees before he took her from behind. His thrusts were hard and fast while he reached underneath her to touch her breasts, pinching her erect nipples. Charli grabbed for the headboard, just an arm's length in front of her. It was rough — more like assault than affection — but it turned her on in ways that surprised her. Grayson hollered out, "Oh God, yes!" in unison with Charli's second meeting with ecstasy this morning. She opened her eyes as she moved to lie down on her back on top of the disheveled bedding. Grayson also was spent on his back, right beside her. And as she lay naked with her husband in the afterglow of rough sex or intense love making, whatever anyone wanted to call it, Charli tried to will herself to stop thinking about Jack Horton.

CHAPTER 6

Jack showed up at home at dinner time with a pepperoni and mushroom pizza. He called Laney earlier to be sure she hadn't a plan for dinner. She spent all morning practice driving with her father, and then he took her out to lunch. *She was getting out,* Jack thought. *Remarkable!*

Laney had the table set and two glasses of red wine poured when Jack placed the large pizza box on the middle of the kitchen table. Laney noticed he brought his laptop home. That wasn't unusual at all, but the fact that he hadn't left it on the wooden bench on his way in the door was out of the norm. She pushed the thought from her mind, for now. Her insecurities about designing with Jack were still a serious issue for her. Her focus now had to be the baby she wanted to conceive. She wanted Jack to deal with his label alone.

"Pizza was the perfect idea for tonight," Laney stated, rolling her wheelchair up to the open spot at the table.

"Good," Jack smiled, taking a sip of wine while Laney lifted the lid on the pizza box. "So tell me about your day. Are you a confident cruiser yet?"

Laney laughed at his comment. "It's not bad. I wasn't at all tense about using the hand gears. It just took awhile for me to relax out there again. Being on the streets of Savannah again, after three long years, affected me. I cried at the intersection where my accident happened. My father was very patient with me and so compassionate, but I know today wasn't easy for him either." Jack sighed at the thought of what Laney really must have gone through today. Then the guilt seeped through him. He should have been the one to be with her for such a huge step. Laney put a slice of pizza on her plate and then Jack reached for her hand.

"I'm sorry. I'm so proud of you though. You're getting out, you're channeling the brave and strong Laney Allison that stole my heart the moment we met," Jack gripped her hand tighter.

Laney laughed, "I was just a girl then, with no bravery or strength in me yet."

"I disagree," Jack stated. Laney's mother had died when she was nine years old. By the time Jack met her, four years later, Laney had already been through terrible loss and still dealt with the ongoing grief. When he heard her story then, Jack believed she was courageous. "I truly am so proud of you."

Laney smiled. "Eat, before the pizza gets cold."

"You love cold pizza," he reminded her.

"Then save me a piece to eat for breakfast," Laney giggled, as she took a generous bite from the cheesy end of the slice in her hand. Even her hefty appetite seemed to have returned.

After Jack poured them each a second glass of wine, he reached for his laptop at the far end of the table. Laney acted as if she didn't notice.

"I got in touch with a potential contact at the factory in New York City today," Jack began, as he flipped open the laptop's lid. "I could have a chance. They're willing to at least get my prototype out there." Laney was aware that was a sample product, a design built strictly to see if it was something that consumers would be interested in buying — and wearing.

"That's wonderful, Jack," Laney told him, and she was being sincere. "I mean, after three years those contacts could have moved on. I'm really happy for you."

"For us," Jack corrected her. For chrissakes, he wasn't some stranger to pat on the back and wish good luck. He was her husband and they were in this together. His career success was also going to be hers. *Wasn't it? Why hadn't she still felt that way?* "I want you to take a look at my top one hundred, but first, I believe I have the design I should use for the prototype. You may think another will work better. Just scroll through all of them," Jack suggested, as Laney tried to her best to appear interested before she looked at his first design.

OBLIGATED

It was a cowl neck cape, or perhaps it would be categorized as a poncho. It was a wrap-front design with significant frayed ends. It was beautiful. Elegant. Classy. It was typical JACK, Laney had thought first. The color he used in this design was bone, and again it was striking. Laney would definitely have worn it, in a time when she could stand up and flaunt it. *Maybe that was part of her problem right now. She had always said she would be the first to model the JACK label. She was proud of the mere thought. From a chair now, who really cared what she was wearing. She certainly did not.*

Jack watched her eyes as she stared at the computer screen. He was sure she was zeroing in on the detail. He was ready for her to be his critic. He learned from her. She was such an asset in perfecting even the smallest feature on his pieces. "It slips over the head, as you can see. Could it use more? Buttons, perhaps? Or just one sizable, prominent button in the center of the neckline, you know at the base where I could make the material gather…" Jack was rambling his ideas. And Laney was completely silent.

She nodded her head. "It's beautiful, Jack. Stunning. Classy. It's so you. Really. You still have it. You haven't lost a single touch of creativity." *He hadn't lost a damn thing. But she had. She couldn't use her damn legs.* A part of Laney was relieved Jack had not chosen trousers or a skirt for his prototype piece. Not that it would have been purposeful, but how insulting nonetheless for her. *Here, yes, allow me to sit down in my wheelchair as I wear, and fail miserably to show off, the first piece my husband designed for the world. What a joke.* Laney wanted Jack to chase his dream, and to achieve the success he deserved. But she no longer desired to be a part of it.

"But what does it need, Lane?" Jack tried not to sound desperate, but it was instantly the way he felt when she gave him no genuine reaction. *Sure, she loved it...but what could he do to make it unique and more JACK?*

Laney stared intently at the piece again. "Not a thing, Jack. It's perfect as it is."

Jack's face fell. This was devastating. They weren't a team anymore. Not in every way. They were obligated to each other as husband and wife, but their shared passion for fashion design was gone. Jack feared what would happen now. He had held out hope for three long years for Laney to eventually come around. He never believed for one measly second that she would give up her talent to create, to sew. *My God, she could still sew from her wheelchair!* Maybe Jack was being insensitive now. He honestly felt so lost that he didn't know what to think, or where to turn. *Should he still go ahead with the design as solely his?* Without Laney, he didn't have as much faith in its success.

"Thanks," he said as he closed the lid of the laptop in front of her.

"Wait? What are you doing?" Laney asked, surprised at him. "I thought I was going to take a look at your top one hundred?" A part of her was relieved that maybe Jack would not expect her to sit there and sift through style after style with his eyes glued on her, attempting to read the emotion in her every expression.

"You just don't seem into it right now," Jack told her, knowing all too well she could see the pain and disappointment in his eyes.

OBLIGATED

"Well, later then. Whenever you're ready is fine with me," Laney told him. Jack nodded as he stood up from the table. He was going to clear their dishes and put the leftover pizza in the refrigerator. *At least Laney was still able to express her like for cold pizza. She seemed to have lost her opinions of everything else.* Jack was being petty, but he was angry now. His hurt quickly turned into a heated, irate feeling rising from the pit of his stomach and settling heavily on his chest.

"I want you to focus on your designs, Jack," Laney spoke as he turned around to place their plates in the empty sink. His back was still to his wife, as she continued to speak. "But, for me, getting pregnant comes first. I bought an ovulation kit today, because, well, I had a hunch. I can still read my body. I'm fertile right now, and I was last night too. The more we try this week, the better our chances will be…" Laney's words trailed off, as Jack finally turned back around from the sink to face her. His face instantly reddened and his eyes pierced hers.

"You want to have sex again? You're asking me to come through for you, to make love to you?" he asked her, and she nodded. "You just crushed the hope I've held onto through everything, the trust I had that one day you would be ready to help me make our designs a success." Laney stared at him in silence. She couldn't remember a time before when she had seen him like this. Angry. Broken. She knew he shattered and unraveled along with her following the accident, but for her sake he concealed his pain in order to pull her through — and give her hope. The hope she needed to prevail.

Laney willed herself to be the courageous woman Jack believed of her, and now defended what she wanted. "You need to have more faith in your talent. I know you feel out of practice, especially with receiving feedback. In college, everyone praised you. You've always been entirely too humble. Show it off, Jack. Share with the world the gift you have."

Jack knew what Laney was doing. She was manipulating him to in order to get her way. She wanted a baby. *Build him up with praise and he'll come around.* He stewed in his anger as he stood there, not moving a muscle. "A part of me wants to walk out of here right now," he told her. "I don't know, to take a drive, to end up in my empty store downtown. But eventually, I would have to come back here and face where we are at in our life. I didn't say our lives, I said our life. We share one life in this house and in this marriage together. And, we used to share one pipe dream."

"It's not a pipe dream!" Laney spoke up immediately.

"I guess we will find out," Jack stated as a matter of fact.

"What does that mean?" Laney asked him, and she felt herself hold her breath.

"It means I'll try. I'll start with the cowl neck poncho and go from there." Jack's excitement for his first prototype was gone. He only wanted to move forward, prepare to accept failure, and then just resume existing with his wife. Like her, he felt he no longer had a purpose. He finally understood Laney's frame of mind. He wasn't confined to a chair, but he was obligated to exist. He would be her husband — and just put up a happy front. *Maybe out of spite he would spend ridiculous amounts of her father's money?*

Laney was having a difficult time reading him. He seemed bitter, but yet he had agreed to pursue his career. Finally. "That's wonderful. We should celebrate!" she offered, smiling, but she felt awkward around him right now. This wasn't at all how they used to be as a couple. They never had a reason to argue, or see the negativity in anything. Real life, and strife, had broken them down.

"We already drank a bottle of wine," Jack stated, bluntly. "That's enough celebrating for me."

And this time Laney was the one who felt crushed. She would reach out to him again later when he was lying beside her in their bed. For the first time in three years, she had an ambition, a reason to seek a more fulfilling life. She wasn't about to give that up. She wanted a baby.

CHAPTER 7

Charli hustled down the outside stairwell. It was exactly eight minutes before Liam's bus was due to arrive. She only had to walk less than two blocks to be at the bus stop before he arrived. It was part of Liam's routine to see her through the bus window from his fourth seat on the right-hand side. As soon as he made eye contact with her, Charli would wave, and then Liam knew it was time to get off of the bus and go home. Something so simple could be extremely difficult if Liam was ever thrown off of his routine. Charli knew all hell would break loose in his little mind if she was not promptly waiting for him after school every morning at that bus stop at five minutes after eleven. Chaos erupted even when she was waiting there for him and nothing had changed. Those were the times Charli would carry her son home kicking and screaming in her arms.

OBLIGATED

She was descending the stairs and level with Vera's apartment when she saw her hanging out of her window again, resting her elbows on the sill. "Good morning, Vera!" Charli spoke first.

"I'd say it's certainly a good morning for you," Vera replied, with a loud, almost obnoxious giggle.

"What?" Charli smiled only because Vera's laugh was hilarious for those familiar with it and knew her well as Charli did. She had this ritual where she opened her mouth wide before any of the laughter came out.

"I get it, honey. I was once young and had a libido that bounced me off the walls sometimes, too. But, these walls in this old building aren't soundproof." Vera made that circular motion with her mouth again before she howled with laughter. And Charli's eyes widened.

She covered her face with both of her hands, muttering "Oh my God," behind her fingers and then she slowly peeked at Vera. "Grayson forgot his cell phone this morning."

"Well where in the Sam hell were y'all looking for it?" More howling laughter.

Charli blushed. "I'm really sorry we disturbed you, Vera."

"Oh nonsense," Vera winked at her from behind the round frames of those dark rimmed glasses. "It makes for a healthy marriage. Never lose sight of how often closeness like that needs to happen, especially while raising a child like Liam. The two of you are always so focused on him and his needs. I'm just saying…" Again, Charli realized what wise advice Vera often had to give. And she took it to heart as she blew a kiss to that mature woman in her life, as she proceeded down the stairs. Vera knew where she was going.

It took several months following the accident before Laney accepted, and actually looked forward to, the routine of having physical therapy every other day. She admitted to her regular in-home therapist how much better she felt after a session. The therapist had told Laney they were going to repeatedly focus on the same goals – to improve her circulation, reduce her fatigue, increase her flexibility, and all of that would improve her overall health. Laney was burdened with paraplegia, but she was a healthy young woman. Vera Faye stressed that point to her all the time.

Vera Faye had forty-four years of experience as a developmental therapist working with children, and as a physical therapist working mostly with accident victims where the focus was rehabilitation and learning to work around injuries. At sixty-six years old, Vera was now only working part-time – and she had gotten very attached to Laney Horton as her patient for the last three years.

When Vera first met Laney, she was a broken young woman. And that was to be expected, given the outcome of her car accident. Her entire life had changed when she was told she would never walk again. Vera wanted to lie down and cry with her. The unfairness of her fate was heartbreaking. But, the professional therapist in Vera knew that if she didn't push that young woman she would lose more than the use of her legs. She would lose herself. Sometimes Vera still was not sure if she had entirely succeeded with Laney. But she continued to try.

Vera stood near Laney as she managed to transition with her upper body strength from her wheelchair to the theracycle. Her goal, first and foremost, was always to encourage Laney to be self sufficient. Today the focus was on her lower body with a machine that was a motor-powered, computer monitored fitness device designed to guide disabled users through a programmed workout. Its sole purpose for Laney was to exercise her legs, and focus on improving flexibility and range of motion. She lost quite a bit of her muscle tone, but nonetheless Laney still had perfectly healthy legs. Instead, the problem resided in her spinal cord, which could not send or receive signals to her lower body due to her injury.

It had only been a few minutes, and Laney was already perspiring profusely. Vera dabbed her forehead with a towel as Laney continued to allow the machine to move her legs. If she wanted, she could close her eyes and imagine her legs were moving all on their own. She opted never to do that though. *Why bother? Because that was false. Her legs would be useless to her for the rest of forever.*

"I've always been a huge sweater, especially when I used to run," Laney offered, appearing to be in an exceptionally good mood, and Vera smiled as she pushed up her dark-rimmed glasses on her nose.

"We can find ways to still make you sweat," Vera teased.

"I used to sweat during sex," Laney admitted, and then giggled. This was the first time Vera could remember her talking so openly about herself. She was more prone to focus on her workout, and talk less. Unless she was complaining.

"Oh my," Vera stated, "I suppose sex when done right can be quite the workout." They both laughed, and Vera kept to herself how her neighbors had gotten it on quite rowdily this morning. *Holy Smokes...*

"Remember when I told you that I want to get pregnant, how I'm so ready to have a baby," Laney caught Vera's full attention as she dabbed her forehead again, and checked the set speed of the machine, contemplating if the pace was too much for her today. Vera left it unchanged. It was good, but very unusual, to see Laney push herself.

Vera nodded her head. "And I also remember telling you that first you need to accept yourself and your life as it is now. Have your loves in order before you bring a child into your life." Laney wasn't entirely sure what Vera meant by that. *She assumed, love yourself first.*

"I'm ready," Laney vaguely stated, leaving Vera to wonder if she meant she was ready to embrace acceptance — or ready to become pregnant. During their last session, she and Laney had talked at length about a very personal subject. Vera told Laney that she was one of the lucky ones in her situation, believe it or not, because she had some feeling below the waist. Having a spinal cord injury could interrupt the communication between the nerves in the spinal cord that controlled bladder and bowel function. That type of dysfunction was never an issue for Laney. Laney had also discovered, while doing her own personal research, that there were nerves associated with sexual pleasure that completely bypassed the spinal cord. She knew she had feeling *down there* at times, and that the idea of having sex again with her husband wasn't entirely out of the question. Even still, they had waited three years.

"I think that's wonderful, if you are sure," Vera stated. "I don't want to pry, but you're acting different. Has something changed?" Vera had her suspicions. Considering how young of a couple they were, Vera was happy for them if they had managed to get creative to enjoy intimacy again.

"Jack and I have finally been able to be close again… physically." Vera could almost hear the sigh of relief come from Laney after she spoke those words. She dabbed her forehead again, and held Laney's face in both of her hands.

"Welcome back to being a woman, honey. I told you that everything was going to take time to relearn or adjust to. I'm really happy to hear your news." Vera often felt great sympathy for the young man who was Laney's husband. He obviously tried very hard to be positive and helpful, but he was only human with needs too. *What a good, ever-patient man.* That had always been Vera's opinion of him.

Jack checked his watch again. He thought the little yellow school bus stopped out there between eight and eight fifteen every morning. He looked out the window and didn't see Charli and her son waiting either.

This was wrong on so many levels. Laney was his best friend, his confidant, his wife. Jack told himself that Charli was just a friend. Something sparked between them because they shared common ground. They understood assisting someone with a trying hardship. That's all.

If that was all, why did Jack go there again last night when he felt Laney reaching for him in the dark, in their bed. She touched him overtop his boxers at first, and then she slipped her hand inside. He responded. *Did he want to risk making a baby? God, he didn't know for sure.* He just knew when he started to think about Charli, while his wife was touching him, he reacted in spades.

Jack closed his eyes and shook his head, trying to push away that feeling, the memory of using those images in his mind to find pleasure while he was with Laney. He never had done anything like that before in his life. He didn't play mind games. It felt wrong, but addictive. If no one knew, there would be no harm in it.

The roar of the bus engine suddenly snapped Jack from his trance. He had missed seeing Charli walk her son onto the bus, but there she was now standing along the side of the cobblestone street, watching it pull away from the curb and drive off. And then she started to walk downtown. *Coffee, he assumed. Or maybe, she would walk by his store again on the opposite side of the street.*

CHAPTER 8

Jack contemplated just walking out of the front door of his store at the same time Charli was near, no matter which side of the street she was on. He had already gotten his coffee fix for the morning, but only he knew that. He walked in circles around his makeshift desk, and just then the door chimed.

"Richard?" Jack's tone sounded as surprised as he felt to see his father-in-law walk into his wanna-be store downtown Savannah. The rental-space that Richard Allison signed the checks for every month.

"Hello Jack. I was in the neighborhood, if you believe that, so I thought I would stop in." Richard was not a big burly man as one might imagine a wealthy and powerful male in his late sixties to be. He was only about an inch or inch and a half taller than Jack at six foot, and his body was round. He had chubby, dimpled hands, a double chin, and a round belly that not even the longest necktie could completely cover. His hair was untouched by father time as it was still full, wavy, and every bit as dark brown as Laney's.

"Of course, anytime," Jack stated, trying to relax. He did see from where he stood that Charli had entered the coffeehouse across the street. This, his father-in-law showing up, was probably a sign. *Get Charli with an I out of your head.*

"Honestly, Jack…I'm here to discuss a few things with you in private." In other words, he didn't want his daughter to know. Jack offered his father-in-law his full attention. "Anything that you need to jumpstart your career — funds, connections, whatever it may be — just ask." Jack stayed silent. *Hadn't this man already done too much? And his generosity still continued.* "I'm happy to hear you are ready to get this business up and running," Richard held up his hands in the empty space where they stood. "I know the turmoil you've been through with Laney. You needed time, just like she did. To see her ready to tackle life again, in a very challenging way, is a prayer answered for me. You may think you owe me, son," Laney had obviously confided in him about Jack's outburst regarding them living off of her father's money, "but really I owe you much, much more. Without you, my little girl would have given up completely." It was rare for Richard to pay anyone a compliment, so Jack was somewhat taken aback — and touched.

"I feel like I should say, 'you're welcome' or 'no problem,' but that just wouldn't be right. I love Laney, I have always loved her. It broke me when she was basically told her life would never be the same again, that she would never be whole. There have been times when I didn't know what to do, so I did nothing. There's really no need to thank me for standing by your daughter's side. I know where I belong." Jack felt slightly hypocritical as he spoke, but up until just weeks ago all of those words would have rang true. *And they honestly still did*, he reprimanded himself. *He was never unfaithful to his wife.*

"Then give her a baby," Richard spoke sternly. That was the Richard Allison whom Jack was better familiar with. He barked orders, and expected obedience.

"With all due respect, that's personal," Jack stated, standing up a little taller.

"It's her incentive. She's finally on the path of wanting to grab ahold of life and live again," Richard defended his initial order for Jack to get his daughter pregnant. "Whatever you need, will happen. A live-in nanny, a bigger house if necessary. Anything."

Jack wanted to interject to say he could not be bribed, but he had been living off of this man's fortune since the day he married his daughter. Instead, he said, "If my wife and I choose to have a family, you will be the first to know, grandpa."

※

He couldn't think of anything else after his father-in-law left. The audacity of that man was not surprising. It was the fact that Laney shared absolutely everything with her father that unnerved Jack. Nothing in their marriage was sacred, or private.

Jack had already emailed his prototype to New York this morning. Now he would wait for the feedback. Acceptance or rejection. He supposed he was prepared for both.

After a failed attempt to focus on designing, he walked outside for some air. And this time, his search for Charli wasn't intentional but he found her.

The bus had already sped off, Jack could see the backend of it a block and a half away. He turned toward the drop-off point, cattycornered from where he stood on the sidewalk of his storefront, and he watched what appeared to be an intense struggle. Charli was down on the ground on both knees, facing her son on his level. Whatever she was saying to him went unheard. The toddler had his hands over his ears and he was repeatedly shaking his head. Jack wondered if he was crying, or maybe repeating the same words over and over as he had remembered seeing on the movie Rain Man. That was the understanding, the only connection Jack could make with Autism. He realized that a movie filmed three decades ago, older than him, was probably not a good comparison for what Charli presently dealt with. He felt for her. He wished there was something he could do to help. He realized many people looked at Laney the very same way. She loathed the stares, the pity, those people who tried too hard to help. Jack questioned if he should even be standing there, obviously watching what unfolded. Charli was the boy's mother. She knew how to handle him. Jack turned to go back inside of the store after looking over his shoulder one more time. Charli had resorted to picking up her son, and walking swiftly away with his little arms and legs flailing.

Charli knew the outburst from Liam was not a *tantrum* or a *conniption fit*, this was a reaction to something that was not right in her son's world. She tried to remind herself of that and sympathize as her eye was watering profusely from being poked, and her neck was bleeding from the claw marks. He was just a little boy, but he could leave some obvious battle wounds on his mother from time to time.

Whether right or wrong, Charli had planted her three year old on the floor in front of the television the moment they walked in the door. She hurriedly scanned the channels while Liam flopped his body around relentlessly on the carpet, still wailing. Charli was relieved to find a black and white episode of Leave it to Beaver. Liam immediately calmed, and Charli left the room to check her wounds in front of the bathroom mirror. She had to work tonight. Guests at the hotel front desk would be sure to wonder about her chafed neck and bloodshot eye. *She could always say she was in a bar fight.*

Her left eye was watering profusely, and she could barely keep it open to take a look at it. She couldn't see anything — no abrasion, no blood. She grabbed a wash cloth from the drawer, ran it under cold water from the faucet, and applied it to her eye. She kept it there while she walked down the hallway and back into the living room to check on Liam.

He wasn't sitting in front of the television, where he was completely content just a minute ago, and panic immediately settled in her chest when she noticed their apartment door was standing wide open. *They never locked it.*

CHAPTER 9

Charli took off running. *The stairs. Liam walks clumsily on his toes.* Not even a second later, she heard screaming.

From the landing at the top of the stairs, outside of their apartment building three stories high, Charli spotted Vera on the ground, hovered over Liam. "Call 911!"

The cell phone that was on the coffee table in the living room was now pressed tightly to Charli's ear as she ran crazily down those steps to get to her son. "Oh my God! He fell, he fell! My son, he's three, we need an ambulance at the apartment complex on Maue Street."

Liam's eyes were open, there were tears on his face, but no sound was coming from him. "I saw it. I had just gotten out of my car. He almost made it down. He wasn't very high up. Is the ambulance on its way?" Vera was talking so fast that Charli had to think before she answered her.

"Yes!" Charli attempted to reach for her son. *Why wasn't he making any noise? Crying? Screaming? Flailing limbs?*

"He's in shock," Vera lowered her voice. "Do not pick him up. Get close, but don't move him. His arm could be broken. He fell completely on it."

Charli brought her hand to her mouth, and suppressed the urge to cry. Her left eye was still watering profusely. She willed herself to hold it together for her little boy. "Liam," she said, trying to get him to make eye contact with her. "Liam, it's mommy. It's okay, you're going to be fine. Does your arm hurt?" She couldn't say they were going to the hospital or the doctor, because Liam feared those places. He had seen his share of doctors and nurses already in his three years of life. To him, they were entirely too up-close and personal. Too intrusive.

She tried not to look at his arm. Charli had a weak stomach. If there were to be a bone poking out of the skin, she'd be a goner. And Vera knew that, which was why she already had her sweater wadded up on the ground and partially covering Liam's potentially broken arm.

The sirens were already approaching the apartment building, and Vera forced Charli's attention on her. "Let the paramedics do their job, but stay close so Liam can see you. Charli nodded. This woman understood her son's reaction to strangers, and better yet Charli's need to overprotect him.

※

Vera followed, in her car, close behind the ambulance. She wasn't sure at this point who she was more worried about, Liam or Charli. When she climbed into the back of the ambulance, making every effort to stay very close by her son, she looked terrified. Liam was still in a serious state of shock. The paramedics confirmed that. The child's pulse was rapid and weak, his skin was cold and clammy, his breathing was shallow, and his eyes appeared to stare.

Sirens close by had caught Jack's attention while he attempted to accomplish something at this desk. He stood up abruptly after he noticed people on the street were eyeing something.

"What's going on?" Jack asked, stepping outside of his store where a group of people gathered at the corner to gawk down the street.

"Someone said a little boy fell from the stairs of that apartment building over there," a woman offered. Jack swallowed hard. *Oh my God. Charli's son.*

OBLIGATED

Charli stood right by the gurney in the emergency room, and Vera was beside her. They were already in a small room, behind a privacy curtain. The nurse had explained that an x-ray for Liam's arm would have to wait. He needed fluid resuscitation to raise his blood pressure quickly. Charli held back the tears when they inserted an IV into her son's vein in his good arm. Other than a flinch, when he tightly closed his eyelids and then opened them again, Liam had not moved. This was not her son. Her son would have come off of that table, fighting mad. Charli was scared. Vera squeezed her hand a couple of times, and whispered just a moment ago, "The fluid and the medication they gave him will bring his blood pressure back up, and he'll come out of this."

Charli nodded. Grayson was on his way. She needed him, but she was afraid to tell him she failed their son. She didn't protect him when she should have. Her husband would blame her, Charli knew that for sure, but it didn't matter as she already felt at fault.

Liam became agitated a few minutes later, so Charli moved closer to him. "It's okay, mommy's here. You are in the hospital." He made some sort of sound that could have been a cry, and Charli smiled. "That's it, you tell 'em. Tell the nurses your arm hurts. That's why we are here, to make it all better." Liam hadn't realized yet, but his arm was restrained — his body was strapped to the gurney — so he would not be able to jolt and further injure himself.

"He's doing fine, mom," the nurse reassured Charli, just as the privacy curtain in their cubby was thrown back, and Grayson hurried to step inside.

He slowed down as soon as he saw his son, strapped to the gurney, with an IV dripping into his arm. He knew better than to speak too loud, or too quickly. Those simple things, even a father wanting to excitedly greet his son when he came home after work, often set him off. How many times did he and his wife emphasize to everyone in their lives, *"Don't say hi, don't say his name. Just exist quietly at first, until he gets used to you being in his space, let him warm up and come to you."*

Grayson stepped toward his wife and son. Vera had taken a few paces back, and was now near the nurse. Charli had given the medical staff a brief overview of her little boy's special needs. *No diagnosis?* They had asked. *Not yet,* Charli responded, and all the while that word *Autism* sounded off in her ears. A part of her wanted it. *Just say that he has it, and then say it again. I need to get used to hearing it, and speaking it. I'm certainly no stranger to it — I know what it entails, I know it's a bitch to decipher most of the time, but I'm doing it, I'm dealing — so why the hell do I hate the mere word so much?*

"He fell," Charli started to explain, "down the stairs outside." Grayson instantly tried to imagine it. He knew Charli always held his hand, or carried him. She had stressed for Grayson to do the same, time and again, when he was alone with Liam. *Those steps are dangerous for any child, much less our unsteady one.* "They think his arm is broken," Charli spoke with her voice low. Liam was listening. He always listened, they knew. He just didn't respond most of the time. "But, he went into shock, so they're dealing with bringing up his blood pressure now." That explained why his son was unusually calm.

A doctor, who Charli had already met in that room earlier, joined them. He remembered not to make a grand entrance, just a quiet one. He nodded at Grayson, and then looked at Charli. "His pressure is nearing normal again. We'd like to get that x-ray done while he's still calm. If not, we may have to sedate him for it." Charli had explained to the doctor how irate and physical Liam could get. She couldn't imagine him lying still and being compliant for the x-ray. And she wasn't sure they would allow her to be by Liam's side for it. If they knew what was good for Liam — and anyone else near him — they would let her lay her body down on the lab table right alongside of her boy.

"Can I go with him?" Charli immediately asked, and the doctor nodded. "Walk along, and the lab technicians will tell you when you must step back. You may remain in the same room with him at all times." Charli heard herself say, "thank you," and the relief in her voice was evident.

Vera and Grayson were the only two people left in the small room now. "I should go," Vera stated. She never did feel comfortable around him. He was a nice looking man with a physique of an athlete, and curly brown hair that made him look boyish. He was a good father, and from what Vera knew he was also a supportive husband, although Charli didn't speak too openly about him that often. To Vera, however, Grayson was arrogant and cocky, and she often wondered how a sweet girl like Charli ended up with him.

"Wait," Grayson stated, as Vera watched him loosen a multi-colored necktie that she thought to be *not very fashionable*, or rather *ugly*. "What happened to Liam today? How did he fall? We both know Charli watches him ridiculously close all the time."

Vera pushed her dark rimmed glasses up on her nose. "It was an accident, those things are going to happen with Liam." She didn't say because he's quirky and clumsy, but what she implied offended Grayson regardless.

"He's growing out of that clumsy stage. He hardly ever walks on his toes now!" Vera took a deep breath through her nostrils. She most certainly was not going to be the one to tell Grayson that Liam was alone on the stairway when he fell.

"You're right," Vera tried to appease him. "The older Liam gets, the easier things will become." *Who was she kidding? Sometimes people like Grayson weren't reachable anyway. May as well feed him a line of bullshit.* "I have to get to work. Charli will tell you what happened."

When Vera closed the curtain behind her, leaving Grayson alone in there, he scoffed under his breath, "Old bitty."

CHAPTER 10

Vera pushed the glass door open as she exited the emergency room. She would catch up with Charli later. She was thinking about how upsetting the last hour and a half had been, but was quick to remind herself how it could have been much worse. It would likely be a challenge for Liam to have his arm in a cast for several weeks, but he would eventually adjust and survive. Vera sympathized with all Charli had already been through as a young mother. She feared she needed an outlet. Between working nights and taking care of Liam, the stress of her life was bound to catch up with her. Vera had a thought. She had done this a few times before when Liam was just a baby. She was going to offer to babysit for an evening very soon. Charli needed a night out, and she hoped Grayson would treat her to one.

Just as Vera stepped out of the door, someone was coming in her direction. Vera held the door for him. She made eye contact to be polite as he did the same. Vera recognized him as the husband of one of her patients. *Laney. Jack!*

Jack thought, *I know her.* She wasn't in her usual attire. Scrubs were her work uniform when she was at the house for Laney's physical therapy. *Vicki, maybe?* Jack was unsure of her name, but definitely recognized her face. "Thank you," he said, now taking ahold of the door. They exchanged a quick *hello, how are you,* and both walked on.

Vera looked back twice before she made it to her car. She didn't see any sign of Laney, unless he dropped her off first and then went to park the car. Vera would have spotted her in the ER's waiting room. It was crowded in there though. Again, Vera hoped Laney wasn't in need of emergency medical care. She had been doing so well lately during her therapy sessions. It was against Vera's oath as a professional therapist to pry. She did wonder though what Jack Horton's emergency was.

Jack sat down, against a far wall where there were a few vacant chairs. He intended to blend with those who also were waiting. Jack could have easily been there waiting for someone. In fact, he was. He wanted to see for himself that Charli's son wasn't hurt too badly from the fall he took down the stairs. He couldn't get the image out of his mind of the paramedics placing his small body on a stretcher, and Charli rushing to climb inside the ambulance with him. He felt like a stalker, eventually following her there. He was being ridiculous. *What would he say if Charli saw him there?* No one popped into the ER just to people watch. He wasn't bleeding, he wasn't doubled over in pain. And he wasn't with anyone. Instead of getting up to leave, a buyers-trade magazine caught his eye on the table beside him. He started to thumb through it because he hadn't read that particular issue yet.

It was at least thirty minutes later and Jack was caught up in an article, but he glanced from it when the door near the check-in window opened.

First, he saw Charli, and in her arms was her little boy. His left arm was in a cast below the elbow. Jack assumed he was lucky to have only broken a bone after falling from a staircase outside of a building. He kept wondering how it happened. *Had Charli been struggling with him? What if she had fallen too?*

Then, he saw a man following behind Charli and her son. He put his hand on the small of her back as they walked quickly through the crowded waiting room. Charli was talking softly into Liam's ear as they made their way to the exit. Jack recalled Charli explaining how much Liam hated unfamiliar settings and strangers. He imagined this ER visit not to have been easy. *So that was Charli's husband.* Jack watched them together. The three of them were a family. It was oddly comforting to see Charli as a part of unit. If he was completely honest with himself, Jack would admit that he was jealous. Not of Charli's husband. Of her having a family. *Maybe Jack wanted a child of his own with Laney afterall.*

Grayson carried Liam up the stairway and into their apartment. He fell asleep during the car ride home from the hospital. The doctor ended up mildly sedating him in order to put the cast on his arm. Liam didn't understand that his arm was broken and he also did not want something on his arm that felt like it was never going to come off. Charli was prepared to explain to Liam, again, why he had to have the cast on his arm, and why he must keep it there for awhile. That would be the battle when he woke up from his nap.

She sat down on the sofa in the living room. *What a day.* It was already early evening, and she was supposed to be at the hotel for the night shift but she had called her boss to explain what was going on and why she would not be in to work. Grayson was unhappy with her for giving up a night's pay. *He was home, he could take care of their son.* Charli insisted she needed to be with their son, too. And that was when Grayson had asked her at the hospital how Liam fell down the stairs. Charli shushed him in front of Liam and one of the nurses. *I'll explain later.*

She rubbed her face with both of her hands. Her eye still felt sore, but it had finally stopped watering. If Charli had looked in the mirror, she would have seen a mildly bloodshot left eye and pink scratches up and down the center of her neck. Grayson had noticed, but he never said anything while they were in the hospital. Now, as he walked into the living room to join his wife on the couch, he was prepared to ask more questions.

His tie was off and his dress shirt was untucked and almost completely unbuttoned. He kicked off his shoes after he sat next to her. "I hope he sleeps for awhile," Grayson stated, "because his arm is probably going to throb for a good day or two. I broke my arm when I was ten, and I still remember how it felt."

"You never told me that before," Charli stated, pulling off her boots one by one. She was still wearing the sweater dress that she had put on this morning. Twice, actually, because Grayson had also taken it off of her. It didn't seem like the same day to either of them. "How did you break it?"

"I fell over the handlebars on my bike. Just being a boy, that's all," Grayson chuckled. One of the things that panged him most though was remembering all of the things he did as a boy when he was growing up, having fun, tempting fate, and getting into trouble. *Would his son ever be able to do, or even want to do, half of the things he did?*

"Do you think Liam will ever learn to ride a bike?" Charli asked her husband and he saw the tears well up in her eyes. She had moments like this, and when she did Grayson never knew how to respond. He was too used to her being the strong one with all of the answers.

Grayson touched her bare knee with his whole hand. "Hey…who knows? You're the one who always tells me we have to take this one day at a time." Charli nodded. "So what happened today? You look like you have some battle wounds. Was Liam fighting you on the stairs when he fell?"

There it was. The moment of truth. The explanation that was going to make Charli feel even worse about Liam being alone and in danger outside on those steep stairs. "He fought me pretty good getting off of the bus. I carried him most of the way. He scratched my eye and it was watering badly when we got in the door, so I put him down on the floor in front of the TV. He was interested in watching Leave it to Beaver, you know how infatuated he gets with those black and white shows. I was only in the bathroom for a minute or two, getting a wet wash cloth," Charli paused, "and when I came back into the living room, the door was open." She choked on a sob.

"What the hell?" Grayson spat at her. "He was on the stairs by himself? You do realize he could have been killed!" Charli nodded her head, and kept fighting the overwhelming urge to sob. "Why didn't you have the door locked?"

"We never lock the door!" Charli defended herself. "Look, I know how bad it was that he fell. I also know it could have been so much worse, but I still feel awful. He's just a little boy and he broke his arm. I can't get past feeling like it was my fault."

"You're damn right it was your fault!" Grayson yelled at her, and Charli was sure Liam would wake up. "I'm always on pins and needles when I'm watching him alone, because you put me there. You and your overprotective rules! I cannot believe you let that happen to him! Jesus Christ, Charli!" Grayson stood up from the couch and paced in front of their coffee table. Charli just sat there, bent forward, wiping her eyes with her fingers. She probably needed to see an eye doctor as her own tears were burning her sore left eye right now, which most likely meant there was an abrasion.

OBLIGATED

"Gray, stop. I feel bad enough," Charli stated, wishing he would leave the room or their apartment for awhile. She wanted space from him. She, however, wasn't going anywhere. She needed to be close to Liam.

Charli got her wish when Grayson stepped outside of their door and stood on the landing to smoke a cigarette. And that's when Charli left the sofa and went into her son's bedroom. He was lying on his back, sound asleep in his little toddler bed that was shaped like a racecar. It was only two feet off of the floor, and the mattress on it was Liam's previous crib mattress. He was still such a baby to her in so many ways.

Charli curled up on the tiny bed, careful not to touch him or bump his casted arm. She could hear him breathing softly. For the first time since he was an infant in her arms, Charli felt like this boy had been a gift to her. Every single breath he took was a blessing. Despite how trying things were with him at times. She could have lost him out there on the stairway today. That accident finally put something in perspective for Charli. *What lied ahead — the challenges, the failed milestones, or just being different — no longer mattered with the same importance to her.* The struggles seemed small to her now. And Charli felt stronger because of it all.

CHAPTER 11

Jack was thinking about Charli's little boy again that evening. Laney had gone to bed early, claiming that her morning physical therapy session was strenuous and she had been worn out all day. He sat in the living room alone, watching the fire in the fireplace. He imagined Charli to have had quite a day. Maybe when they would bump into each other again, she would tell him about it. He debated if he would admit to hearing the sirens and tell her how he ended up in the emergency room — out of what? *Concern?* Jack remembered how he felt when he left the ER. He was beginning to open his heart to the idea of having a baby with Laney. He had not said as much to her, but he wondered if she was already pregnant. If she was, he needed to get a job.

Jack reached for his cell phone on the chair next to him. His contact at the factory in New York had said he would *let him know in a day or two* if there was an interest in his prototype. No new messages, texts nor emails, had come through. Jack looked at the time on his phone. It was twenty-five minutes before nine o'clock. The coffeehouse was still open for almost another hour and a half. He didn't want to wait until morning.

The evening with Liam was not as bad as Charli had feared. He did want his cast off, more than a few times, but he finally seemed to understand when Charli explained that his arm needed to have the cast covering it right now, just like he needed his blankie to cover him every night. That seemed to comfort him, and Charli had caught a smile from Grayson as she came up with the creative analogy for their son. He didn't seem to be upset with her anymore.

Once Liam was tucked into bed, Charli walked out into the living room and found Grayson sprawled on the sofa. His hair was still wet from showering. Those loose curls all over his head could have used a trim, but Charli believed it was a part of his character and charm. He tried to be tough, but really he was often times as soft as those sandy brown curls. That's what she loved most about him. He allowed her to see his softer, kinder side.

"Hey," Grayson said to her as she made her way over to the sofa. She was going to sit down on the end, near his bare feet. She knew he was only wearing boxer shorts underneath that fleece blanket. It's what he always did after showering at night.

"Hey yourself," she responded, still slightly unnerved with him for lashing out at her when she needed to be comforted.

"Do me a favor?" he asked.

"Do I owe you for something?" she was partly teasing.

"No, of course not. I just really need a cigarette, and I'm out. Will you run downtown to the convenience store? You're still dressed." Grayson looked like a child to her now.

She giggled. And she actually suddenly had an idea that appealed to her. "I will get you your fix, and while I'm out I'm going to get mine, too!"

Grayson groaned. "You and that damn coffee."

"You and that damn nicotine," Charli laughed, as she stood up, and pulled on her boots over by the door. With her wristlet in hand now, she turned around to Grayson, gave him a wink, and told him she would "be right back."

※

Jack stood at the cash register waiting for his iced caramel mocha. He chuckled to himself at the thought of how some men indulged in booze while he preferred doctored up, modified coffee. A tap on his shoulder interrupted his comical thought. He turned around to find Charlie smiling at him.

"Hey there," she said first, "looks like we both had the same idea."

"Well hi, yeah who wants to wait until morning," he grinned. *What were the chances for them to once again be at the same place at the same time?*

OBLIGATED

Jack's iced caramel mocha was ready, and Charli glanced at the college kid behind the counter, ready to take her order. He had curly hair the same color as Grayson's, only shorter. "A vanilla latte please," she requested.

"Do you have a minute, or are you in a hurry to get back?" Jack asked her. He did wonder how she managed to get away given the fact that she spent a portion of the day in the emergency room with her son.

"Um, yeah, maybe just a minute," Charli replied, thinking of Grayson waiting for his cigarettes.

They sat down together again at the vacant high table in front of the window. Charli felt uneasy as she claimed one of the chairs. She really had to get going, but yet she wanted to stay. She wanted to talk to him.

"How are things on your end?" Charli asked him as she took a generous sip of her latte.

"Not too bad," Jack answered her, "but I don't want to take up our few minutes rambling about myself. Tell me what's going on with you."

Charli sighed. "You may be sorry you asked. Liam fell down the stairs on the outside of our apartment building today. I'll spare you the long, terrifying details because he's going to be okay. He does have a broken arm. I learned a hard lesson from it. From now on, our door stays locked." Jack immediately gathered the fact that the little boy escaped the house alone and fell. *Yes, how terrifying.*

"I heard the sirens from my store," Jack surprised himself at how honest he was with Charli. It never failed. He wanted her to know the truth. *His thoughts. His feelings.* "The onlookers outside said a boy had fallen from the stairs. I saw you get into the ambulance with him." Charli momentarily closed her eyes. She would never forget this day. "Please don't think I'm a weirdo or a stalker, but later I went to the ER to see if I could find out how your son was doing."

"You did?" Charli asked. She didn't think oddly of him. She was touched. "I don't think they give out that kind of information, do they?"

Jack shook his head. "No, I wasn't dumb enough to ask. I just sat down in the waiting area, hoping I don't know... to see you." Charli waited for him to continue. "I felt foolish for following you and I was actually just going to leave, but I got caught up in a trade magazine for a few minutes. And then you came out, walked through the waiting room, and left. I had my answer. Your son was hurt, but he was going to be okay, which meant I knew you were going to be just fine too." Charli wanted to reach out and touch his hand on the table. *Just a friendly, so grateful for his kindness, squeeze.* But she did not. "I saw you with your family. Beautiful. The three of you look good together."

"You are something else, Jack Horton," Charli finally spoke. "Thank you for caring."

Jack smiled. "I'm glad he's okay, and you too."

"You want to hear something strange?" Charli had not told anyone this. It just didn't feel right to blurt it out to Grayson yet. Half the time he wasn't listening to her anyway. Jack nodded in anticipation. "I feel like today taught me something. Things can get really stressful sometimes and my uncertainty about life and the future could consume me, if I'd let it." Jack understood that feeling in spades. "But today I realized that I can handle it. I feel stronger. Give me those days that I thought were rough, because they really are nothing compared to the panic that runs through a person when you think you've lost someone you love."

"Believe me, I get that," Jack stated, and Charli suddenly felt ridiculous. And foolish.

"Oh my God, I'm sorry. I'm an idiot. Like you don't know!" Charli ceased eye contact with him. She chose to stare down what was left of her latte.

"Hey, it's fine," Jack forced her eyes back to him, simply by speaking. "Haven't you caught on by now? That's what connects us. We live similar lives, just with different obligations."

Charli locked eyes with him. And then her cell phone sounded in the side pocket of her wristlet on the table near her.

"I know you have to go," Jack acknowledged the fact that she needed to get back to her boy — and her husband who was likely waiting for her.

"I really do," Charli said, abruptly standing up. She didn't want to. She had to.

"I'll walk out with you," Jack offered. "I wasn't planning to stay anyway, just a to-go fix."

She held the door for him, as he walked directly behind her. His hand unintentionally brushed hers as she reached for the glass door. It was sudden and instantly over with. The feeling lingered though. *For Jack. And for Charli.* They stepped out into chilly night air, under a dark sky lit with only the full moon and a half a dozen twinkling stars.

"It was really nice to run into you again," Charli admitted, as she was about to turn right, in the direction of the convenience store.

"I completely agree," Jack replied, as he was about to turn the opposite direction toward his parked vehicle along the curb.

And that's when he reached out his arm. His hand touched the side of her cheek. He held his open palm there for a moment. "Take care, Charli with an I."

She blushed, but hoped he wouldn't notice with only the street light above them illuminating the sidewalk they stood on. "You too, Jack."

He walked one way, she walked the other. That was it. It was innocent. It was a sporadic gesture, a soft touch, between friends. Two people who found a common ground. It was platonic, but it didn't look that way at all from across the street.

Vera Faye donned her pale pink sweatsuit and fluffy white ear muffs nightly, after dark, when she walked the block that was the centerpiece of downtown Savannah. She had actually stopped in place to be sure of what she was seeing. Who she was seeing together.

Charli? And Laney's husband, Jack?

Vera's mind flashed back to leaving the emergency room today. Jack was going in—alone. *Was he there because of Charli?*

And then… she remembered this morning when Charli said Grayson came home from the bank because he had forgotten his cell phone. *Was that true?* She never actually saw who came or went from the apartment above her own.

Vera watched the two of them go their separate ways in the dark. She wondered how in the world she would let this go, as she feared people were going to get hurt.

CHAPTER 12

Jack was awake, showered, and dressed early. He then found Laney in the spare bedroom which they had converted to a workout area, specifically for her therapy and recovery. Her long dark hair was knotted up in a high ponytail, and she was wearing black yoga pants and a fitted white tank top, sans a bra. This was new for Laney. It was obvious to Jack that his wife was feeling confident in her own skin again. She was sitting in her wheelchair, lifting hand weights.

"Hey, good morning beautiful," Jack stated from the open doorway. He could hear music playing from her cell phone on the bench press machine in the corner that he probably should start using again.

Laney turned around. "Morning. Did you sleep well?"

"I did. You?" Jack asked.

Laney nodded. "I'm hoping to do a little more of this each day," Laney referred to the weights, "you know like on my own as well as with my therapist, and then maybe I will not be so tired in the evening."

"That sounds like a good idea, but take it slow so you don't overdo it," Jack stated. He still worried about her. He wanted her to be proactive in her recovery. It would help her state of mind. Even still, he felt protective of her and how much she could physically handle.

Laney nodded again. "I heard you leave last night," she told him. She was lying in bed when the turnover of his pickup truck engine surprised her. Her cell phone had been on the charger on top of the kitchen counter, otherwise she would have texted him. "I must have fallen asleep again, because I never heard you come in." When she woke up this morning though, he was beside her.

"A late-night coffee run," Jack smiled.

"Maybe then you should have something different this morning?" Laney suggested, and Jack had considered it. But then he wondered if Charli would be back there, at the coffeehouse. He decided on coffee for breakfast again.

"Yeah maybe. I'll grab something after I get to the store. Is there anything you need, or want?" Jack asked her, before he planned to leave for the day.

"No, I can manage. I have the van if so," Laney reminded him.

"Right," he said, still feeling uneasy about her driving alone. "Be safe in that."

She muffled a giggle at his words. "Really Jack? I think the worst already happened to me when I was behind the wheel." She truly was partly teasing, but Jack didn't take it that way.

"Stop. You can't honestly believe that. The worst that could have happened would have been you not surviving the crash." Jack couldn't imagine his life as complete without her. Maybe he needed to remind himself of that.

His feelings were so jumbled in his mind right now. He loved his wife. He was incredibly proud of her, especially lately as she had shown serious initiative to get better and be stronger. He also was wrapped up in the prospect of finally becoming a designer. If his prototype was accepted, he had a lot of work to do to prepare the world for the first showing of JACK. And then there was Charli who weighed on his mind too much lately. They had a connection. Jack was trying not to read too much into exactly what that meant. He had female friends in his life before, but none like Charli. He always considered Laney to be his confidant all the while she was his girlfriend and later his fiancé. As his wife, however, things changed. They had lost the ability to confide in each other and communicate. And that was because so soon after they were married, Laney's accident changed everything for them.

Jack walked closer to Laney, as she took turns lifting what he noticed were five-pound weights. She stopped and rested both dumbbells on her lap when he knelt down beside her. "I love you," he said to her, and he softly kissed her lips. Laney's aggressive response took him by surprise. She kissed him full on the mouth as she wrapped her arms around his neck and closed any space that was between them. Their bodies were seductively pressed together.

"What is it, Jack?" Laney asked, as she sensed him pull away from her prematurely. She wondered if his nerves were getting the best of him as he awaited news on his prototype.

He backed out of their embrace. "I'm just really happy to see what you're doing for yourself lately, that's all."

Laney smiled. She was making herself happy too. "Oh, and here I thought it was the fact that I'm not wearing a bra."

Jack laughed out loud. Her sense of humor was back. "That, too! Keep that little number on until I get back home." Jack waved his finger at her, and he could still hear Laney giggling as he walked out of the room and down the hallway in search of his Converse by the front door.

Charli was surprised by how the broken arm wasn't even an issue with Liam. He functioned with the cast as if it was a part of him all along. She shook her head at how life with Liam could often be. The big things that she stressed over were sometimes not an issue at all. And then there were the minor things that turned into fiascos and Charli drove herself crazy if she tried to figure out why.

There was a brief conniption fit in the living room when Vera stopped by to see Charli. Her soft knock on the door, which was purposeful because she knew how Liam hated the sound of a doorbell and also feared who was behind the door, had alarmed him to the point of head banging against the wall.

Charli managed to calm her son down in his bedroom. *She told him twelve times that it was only Vera who knocked on the door, she was their neighbor, and wanted to talk to mommy about something.* A part of Charli cursed Vera for not calling ahead to give her notice that she was coming over. She knew how Liam reacted to visitors.

When she walked into the living room, Charli found Vera seated on the end of the sofa. "I'm sorry that I upset him," she immediately apologized.

"It's fine," Charli tried to brush it off. "Everything okay with you?" It was rare for Vera to visit their apartment, one floor up. She used to stop by much more when Liam was a baby. Older women liked to cuddle babies. Playing on the floor with toddlers came in a close second place. With Liam, however, there wasn't much interest in playing. He lined up a lot of his toys, repeatedly. He also spent hours staring at photographs — some in various magazines, and on the covers of books or DVDs.

"Yes, I'm just plugging along. Work keeps me busy." Vera thought of Laney. She had a therapy session with her scheduled for later this morning.

"I took last night off," Charli explained, "but I'm working tonight." When Charli mentioned *last night*, the image of her with Jack Horton flashed into Vera's mind. An intimate touch on the cheek shared between two married-to-other-people adults was inappropriate. That's all there was to it in Vera's mind. She knew the thrill of crossing the line, overstepping boundaries. Maybe it was time she shared that with Charli.

"So you and Grayson had a night in together," Vera stated, not exactly sure how she was going to ease into this conversation subtly. "That's rare for you two, I mean because you work opposite hours and well you're never given the chance to have a date night." Charli watched Vera's face. She believed she knew where she was going with this.

"We don't go out, Vera, for two reasons. One, we have no extra spending money. And two, we have Liam. He's not your typical kid to hire just any babysitter for."

"I understand on both accounts," Vera stated, nodding her head. "I am offering to sit with Liam anytime though. I think he would do just fine with me." Charli had a few doubts about that, but she didn't totally rule out the idea.

"That's sweet of you, Vera. Thank you." Charli was touched that she offered. Most of the people in their lives these days never wanted to get too close.

"Consider it sometime. Have your husband take you out on the town. A date night." Vera may have been pushing it with that, because she watched Charli frown at her before she spoke.

"What's gotten into you? You know my husband. Date nights?" Charli still had a frown on her face.

"Well from what I heard, um, what went on the other morning right above my easy chair by the television..." Vera's implication was understood as Charli laughed out loud.

"Okay, okay, so he's not romantic but we are still mutually attracted to each other." Charli grinned.

"And that's a wonderful thing, honey. I'll admit there are things I miss about being married. The closeness, for sure. Not so much sex. I don't think about sex at my age. Just companionship. Someone to eat dinner with, watch a television show with. Take a drive with. Just those little things."

Charli felt sorry for her. She was lonely. "Oh Vera, I've never thought about that before. How many years has it been since your husband died?" Charli knew that Vera never had any children, but she hadn't thought of her as lonely. She still worked. And she had the most likable personality to befriend anyone.

"Oh, he didn't die. We are divorced. He's remarried actually," Vera clarified.

"I didn't know that," Charli admitted, and she instantly wanted to ask what happened to sever their marriage. But she didn't have to when Vera began to share her story. And that was Vera's intention all along. If she told her story, maybe then she could keep Charli from making a grave mistake.

CHAPTER 13

Charli briefly left the living room to check on Liam, who was quietly lining up stacks of old pictures she had recently found and given to him. The thrill for Liam was many of them were black and white. That *game* sometimes kept him busy for hours. *On a good day.*

"Sorry, go on. He's fine," Charli stated, but Vera waved her hand back and forth in front of her face as if to dismiss the unnecessary apology before she resumed her story.

"So I'm sure you are curious as to why I ended up divorced," Vera began. "I was young and careless, if you consider forty-four years old young. I do, now that I'm another two decades older." Vera laughed, but she tried to muffle the howl behind the palm of her hand as she knew loud laughter alarmed Liam. "We had been married for eighteen years. I was a therapist full time then and he was a police officer for the City of Savannah. Neither one of us ever wanted children. We had our careers, and for a long time we had each other and that was enough. Saul was not the most attentive man in the world, but I knew he loved me. I just lost sight of that, and of how much he truly meant to me – when I met Mac."

"Who's Mac?" Charli interjected, as she feared Vera's answer.

"At first, he was a friend who listened like no one else in my world did at the time," Vera attempted to explain. And Charli already understood. "It only happened one time, but I cheated on my husband. I confused the close connection of friendship with love, or lust, or something that I thought I had a need for. I knew the moment I gave myself to another man that I had made the biggest mistake of my life. And that I did. I lost my husband and my life as I had known it for most of my adulthood. I also lost someone that could have been a good friend to me for life, but we crossed that boundary. It was the absolute stupidest thing I've ever done."

Charli was stunned into silence. This was unbelievable. *Vera cheated.* And here she was telling her this story now. If she had known about Vera's history, before she met Jack Horton just weeks ago, it may not have had such a profound effect on her. Charli believed she would never cheat on Grayson. They had a son together who needed them both. They were in this for life, committed to each other and a marriage they vowed to respect and nurture. *Charli had reminded herself of all of those things many times lately.*

"I'm not sure what to say," Charli spoke honestly. "Please don't take that as if I'm judging you. I certainly am not. I can see on your face how regretful you are about your choice. I know it was many years ago, but I feel terrible for you. One mistake cost you everything."

"You got that right, honey. If only I had thought twice," Vera told Charli.

※

Jack walked in the door at home. He spent his usual several seconds taking off his Converse and kicking the shoes underneath the wooden bench against the wall. A part of him thought about just sitting down there for a few minutes to process everything. *He lived in a home he didn't really own. He was married to the love of his life, and considering he almost lost her, he truly was grateful for the second chance. At the same time, he was angry at her fate. She didn't deserve limitations and that chair for the rest of her life.* At twenty-five years old, Jack needed a compass. He had no direction for his life. Becoming a designer was something he had to go after with his whole heart and soul, or not at all. Jack knew the design he submitted for his prototype was good. It just wasn't good enough. His contact from New York had called him today. *Your submission was rejected. You have potential though. Try again. Forward, in bulk, fifty to a hundred more of your designs and we'll take another look.* But Jack didn't know if that was what he wanted to do.

Not entirely used to seeing Laney's new minivan on the driveway yet, Jack never noticed that it was missing when he parked his pickup a few moments ago. He did observe how the house was unusually quiet. He called out Laney's name twice to no answer. He looked at his watch and it was quarter after five, which was the time he most often arrived home every evening. Jack thought about texting her, but the idea of it being a distraction while she drove led him to decide otherwise.

Ten minutes later, Jack's worry peaked. He had been in the kitchen, and throughout the rest of the house, looking to make absolute sure Laney had not left him a note. *Did anyone still leave handwritten notes?* All Laney would have had to do was call or send him a text, if she had made plans to be out. He gripped his cell phone in his hand as he walked down the hallway, toward the front door again. He considered sitting back down on that wooden bench to put his shoes back on so he could head out to look for her. Just as he was about to do that, he heard someone outside and he watched the door handle turn from the inside. He pulled on the door from his end. Laney was about the roll over the threshold. "Oh hey!" she said to him, "thanks for getting the door. It's a bitch with this chair." She giggled and Jack was so taken aback by her positive and suddenly cocky attitude that he just stood there, taking it all in. The questions he had — like, for one, *where've you been,* and two, *what's in the bags on your lap* — were lost to him as he just felt happy. *Happy to see her like this.*

OBLIGATED

Jack snapped himself out of the stare as he reached for whatever she needed help with on her lap. "Oh yeah, take those please," she began to explain. "I picked up Chinese for dinner."

"You did? You're serious?" Jack asked, and now he could smell the food. His mouth watered at the thought of the salty taste of fried rice and egg rolls. He hadn't eaten all day. The news from New York had robbed his appetite. But now, he wasn't thinking about rejection or the future or anything at all except for how evident this moment was for him. It meant something he couldn't even put words on. It was just the two of them and this moment felt normal — and so fulfilling. Laney was finally doing things she had to work a thousand times harder for than she used to, but she grasped the accomplishment with a smile and an attitude that had been lost to her for years. It was just Chinese take-out, but to Jack it was so much more. He wondered if she was half as proud of herself as he was of her at this moment.

"You're staring," Laney spoke as Jack stood in front of her in the hallway, still by the door she had just closed behind her moments ago.

Jack held the take-out bags in his hand. "Sorry. It's just that you really are something. I could have picked up the food on my way home. But you did it, Laney. You did it!"

Laney smiled. And then she laughed out loud. Her eyes were bright. She knew the feeling that was racing through Jack's veins right now. She felt it even more so. It didn't matter that it took her fifty-five minutes to leave the house to run one errand and return with take-out, and both places were less than five minutes away. *All that mattered was she did it!*

Jack was oblivious to the fact that he was holding take-out in one bag, and a home pregnancy test in the other.

CHAPTER 14

"So was it positive?" Charli asked, as Jack confided in her about last night. He had not known what was in the bag from the drugstore. Not until later that evening when Laney was hunkered down again inside of her shell of self pity. He didn't understand the sudden turnaround in her emotions until she broke down and told him that her period had been two days late, but a home pregnancy test result was negative. Jack attempted to reassure her that they were young and had many months ahead of them to keep trying to conceive a baby. *Not everything happened on the first try.* Jack had thought of his prototype which had failed on the first attempt. Laney had been too upset about not being pregnant that he refrained from telling her. *It just wasn't an appropriate time.* And now, a storm had blown in quicker than Charli expected when she was walking en route to the coffeehouse. The sky was gray and the wind had picked up, but she thought she had time to walk there and then back home. She was grateful to have gotten Liam on the bus before they were both soaked from the merciless rain. While the winds blew crazily outside of Jack's store window, Charli was relieved to have sought shelter when she did. *Would she rather have been across the street with a cup of latte in her hand?* Choosing between anything and Jack was getting more difficult to do.

They were seated on the bare floor with their backs against the wall. Jack had offered Charli his only chair in the unfurnished space, but she declined and opted for the floor. And then he joined her. "No," Jack replied and shook his head, in reference to the results of the home pregnancy test, "and Laney was beyond upset. She literally went from ready to tackle anything ahead of her in this world to broken and unreachable. It's so tiresome, Charli. Her hope is fragile and very easily crushed. It was one month. We had sex twice, that's it. It's not like there's a problem. We will just try again." Charli willed herself to kick that image out of her mind. *Sex. Sex with Jack.* She didn't mean to, but she caught herself envisioning it. *Them. Jack and his wife.* Charli had never met her. She had no idea what she even looked like. Even still, she had this image of *her* with Jack. And Charli wished Jack had not brought it up. "She overreacted, big time," Jack added.

"I understand why you would think that," Charli began, trying to focus on what Jack needed from her right now. He needed a friend, not another woman. "I also can see how easy it would be for your wife to feel let down. I mean, to be fair, let's look at this from her perspective. Life robbed her in the worst way. She cannot get up and walk. She is incapable of doing what you and I take for granted when we wake up in the morning and we do not think twice about getting from point A to point B all day long." Jack listened raptly. It was not as if he hadn't thought of any of that before. It just had such clarity coming from another person. Especially from Charli. He respected her opinion more each time they confided in each other. "And with that said, you've told me how Laney recently has had a better grip on mind over matter. That's because she had a purpose, a mission to get pregnant. Her new focus was helping her to seize the day again, and then another let down smacked her in the face. Sure, there's always next month or the month after that but she's living moment to moment, struggling to stay focused on her newfound hope. And then another blow hit her. That just sucks, if you ask me," Charli appeared to conclude what she had to say, and Jack turned his body sideways to look at her. She was sitting close to him. He could have reached out to touch her hand, or her leg. But he did not.

The rain was coming down at a slant outside of the storefront window. The wind was so gusty, he couldn't see across the street. It was as if they were in their own little hideaway. No one could see in, or out. "I need to be more compassionate," he began. "While I've tried to put myself in her place, I haven't fully grasped how easily things can disappoint, or even crush her. I realize that now, because of what you just said. Thanks, Charli."

"You're welcome, Jack." Charli looked away from him now. She started to glance toward the window at the rainstorm which wasn't letting up any, but instead she eyed Jack's Converse. She chuckled a little.

"What?" he asked, and grinned. Even in the gloomy, poorly lit store, he could see how her bright her blue eyes were.

"Your shoes," she stated.

"My all-stars? It's the only kind I ever wear." Today he wore them with loose fitting khakis again. He pulled up his pant legs, both at the same time now, and Charli could see they were high tops. The silly, meaningless question she had asked herself weeks ago now had a definite answer.

"I saw them one time, on your feet, while I waited in line at the coffeehouse," she admitted. "I don't know why, but they caught my eye. And then, from the ground that day when you ran across the street after you thought I could have been hurt on the curbside, I looked down and saw those same shoes. What does it mean, Jack? What does *this* mean?"

Jack paused. "I'm not sure what you're asking me," he replied. *But really, he did know what she was referring too — because he felt it too.*

"You've said before we became fast friends, and I agree. When things have gotten overbearing in my life, you've lifted the weight off of me. Just talking to you brings me this sense of peace that I cannot even put words on. I just feel like you understand."

"That's because I do understand. I get it, Charli. And I think you know you've done all of the same for me. I don't have too many active friends in my boring life anymore. It's just nice to know our paths are prone to cross on those cobblestone streets, or inside of that crack house, oh I mean coffeehouse." They both laughed out loud.

Charli agreed. It was *nice*.

"We've only talked about me since you got here," Jack spoke again, as Charli grew quiet, as if there was something more on her mind. Something else she wanted to say to him. "How are things at home? Is Liam's arm bothering him?"

"The cast is not an issue at all, thank God," Charli clasped her hands together. "He's been his usual roller coaster of emotions self, but otherwise okay. It's Grayson that I cannot handle sometimes." Jack waited for her to tell him why her husband wasn't currently on her most-grateful-for list. "He researches things — everything. Whatever it is, he's convinced there is a solution out there just waiting to be discovered. Problems are solvable, right?" Charli turned to Jack. "Not when it comes to our son. Gray wants to try what the very latest studies have shown to work — for some children. There's a new brain balance therapy out there for behavioral issues, processing trouble, attention deficit disorder, and I don't even know what else. I just quit listening. I am so tired of wasting money we do not have on things that I know will not work. Every child on the spectrum is different. What my gut tells me to do for my son, I'm already doing. And right now, that is to meet his needs. He's only three years old. If he's resisting a new and different therapy that my husband just wants to give a shot to, his whole world will be affected. He regresses. He'll quit saying the very few words he does say. He'll start wetting his pants again when I'm so close to being successful at potty training him. He will lash out until he's spent," Charli sighed. "I may be the one who's wrong here, but I don't feel so in my heart. And I know why. It's because I've accepted my son as different. I'm not grasping at chances to cure him and turn him back into a normal child. He never was average or ordinary. He's Liam. So why can't my husband just love him as he is?"

Jack thought for a moment before he answered her the best way he knew how. "Just as you got inside my wife's head a moment ago, I am going to offer you a similar perspective from your husband's point of view, if I can," Jack began. "A man has an obligation to his wife. Aside from love and respect, he is her protector. And when something goes wrong, he wants to fix it. Men are wired that way. Be the hero. Be her go-to when something is wrong. Be her answer. Grayson does not have the answers for the son the two of you share, so he's hell-bent on being proactive and he's trying very hard to find something to make this right. For Liam. And for you. But perhaps he is trying too hard."

"And here I am being too hard on him for something he's doing for me and our son. For our family," Charli sighed so deeply that Jack watched her chest rise and fall. "Look at us. Look what we've done for each other today. You are going to go home to Laney feeling more patient and understanding with her as she learns how to accept temporary defeat and hopefully bounce back quicker. And I am going to go home to Grayson, more aware of why he does what he does. It's for me." Charli smiled at him. "These talks are beyond good for our souls."

Jack nodded his head in complete agreement. "I could not have said it better myself. Wow. You and I..." Charli's eyes widened and she felt her heartbeat quicken. There was no *you and I* between them. But a part of her liked how it sounded. "We were put in each other's paths for a reason, don't you think?" *Oh yes. She most definitely believed so.* "If I walked out of here and never came back. If my time were up tomorrow, there's something I want you to know." Charli's hands immediately felt clammy. She was nervous. They were alone in his empty store. The storm was beginning to calm. And she needed to leave there. But she didn't want to. And that's what made her feel most unsettled as Jack spoke so softly she almost had not heard his words. "In another time, another place, in a story where there might not be a Laney or a Grayson, I'm certain that I would stop at nothing to be with you."

OBLIGATED

Charli met her eyes with his. She no longer felt frazzled. The sound of his voice had a way of putting her at ease. She was taken in by his every word. "In another story, I believe that would be effortless," she responded with only what was in her heart, before she stood up and walked over to the storefront window. The storm had finally passed.

CHAPTER 15

"I want to make a doctor's appointment," Laney told Jack almost the moment he walked in the door.

"Okay, what's wrong?" Jack immediately asked her. Doctors, specialists, therapists, all unfortunately had become such a way of life for them the past three years.

"I have to tell my gynecologist what's going on, that I wasn't able to get pregnant when I know I was ovulating. I bought the kit for accuracy." Jack thought of when he told Charli that her husband seemed to be hell-bent on being proactive in his research to find the *cure* for his son's disorder. He believed Laney also was hell-bent in her mission to become pregnant. And, like Charli, Jack found it tiresome.

"Laney," Jack tried to sound compassionate and patient, "it was one month. We have to give it more time. Any doctor will tell you that. Let's mate like rabbits next time and see what happens."

Laney laughed. God how he wanted to see more of that from her. *Just relax and live. Have fun.* Jack had an idea.

"I think we should get your mind off of this for a little while. Let's go out to dinner. What do you say? It'll be something different for us," Jack suggested. Take-out had become a constant for them. Dining out had not happened at all since Laney's accident.

"Oh, I don't know. I don't have anything cute to wear… and come on Jack, it's been so long. What if there's no wheelchair ramp? What if people stare? I mean, I'll need the dining chair removed from the table to be able to park mine near it. I'll be a nuisance. I'll be like a circus act, all eyes will be on me."

"Eyes will be on you because you're beautiful, Lane. So what if people glance your way. So what if I have to pull your chair away. I'll do whatever you need to feel comfortable and we can both enjoy something different. A night out. What do you say? Yes? Please…"

Vera noticed that Charli seemed preoccupied when she stopped at her window while on the stairs again. Grayson had just gotten home from work and Charli had the night off from working at the hotel. And right now she was headed to the grocery store for last-minute dinner ingredients. She had to wait until Grayson could stay at home with Liam because going to the store had recently become too overwhelming for him.

"Where are you headed, honey?" Vera leaned her upper body out of the window again.

"Dinner ingredients," Charli smiled. "I have the night off because I worked the last two." For that, Charli was relieved. She needed to catch up on some sleep.

"I have a better idea," Vera spoke up.

"Oh yeah? And what would that be?" Charli hoped it wouldn't be for her to share something homemade. Last time, she and Grayson ate Vera's chili, they had to split a half gallon of milk to wash away the after effect of all the chili powder she had dumped into it. *"This shit is gritty,"* Grayson had quipped.

"Let me watch Liam while the two of you go out to dinner," Vera suggested. "I have a gift card for that new Mexican restaurant. One of my patients gifted it to me and you know how I feel about Mexican food. It goes right through me."

Charli laughed. She and Grayson both enjoyed Mexican food. Dining out, however, was never on their radar because it was too expensive. "That's not necessary, Vera. But, thank you."

"You can thank me after you enjoy a date night with your husband. Go on, tell him you're going out. Give Liam his bath, put him in his jammies, and all I'll have to do is entertain him until bedtime." Vera did have a good plan in mind. Nothing would be different for Liam along the lines of bathing or getting undressed or dressed – both for which he needed help. He could just play or hang out with Vera. If something went wrong, she and Grayson could come right back home.

"I love you, Vera. Do I tell you that enough?" Charli looked at her sincerely and smiled, feeling as if she could get really teary at any moment.

"And I love you like a daughter. Now get back up those stairs and I will see you in an hour." Vera clapped her hands together, feeling very proud of herself.

Laney was doing this for Jack. For all he had done for her the past three years. He rarely asked anything of her, so when he wanted to take her out to dinner for the first time in what felt like forever, she said yes. *For him.*

She chose a cowl neck burgundy knit dress that ended just above the knee. She wore a pair of brown suede boots that actually went over the knee. It was a chilly night, so those boots felt perfect. Her hair was down on her shoulders and she had taken a little time to curl it. Loose bouncy curls were Jack's favorite look. Since Laney felt like this evening was for Jack, she told him to choose the restaurant.

Charli pushed Laney's wheelchair up the ramp right outside of the new Mexican restaurant on Brefeld Avenue. She held her head up high as someone politely propped open the door for them.

"Table for two?" the hostess asked, and it meant so much to Laney for the middle-aged, petite Mexican woman to make eye contact with her, to ask her a specific question. "Yes please." She mattered. She wasn't being treated like an invalid.

When they reached their table, Laney watched Jack take one of the chairs away. He made no mention of it. He just tucked it closer to another chair on the opposite side of their table. The hostess nodded, and offered to bring them a drink while they waited. Jack looked at Laney first. *Ladies first.* That was one of the things she always loved about him. He was a boy with manners who grew into a man who knew how to respect a woman. "I'll have a margarita, no salt," Laney had a mischievous look in her eyes and Jack muffled a chuckle. "That sounds so good. Same for me, please."

Two tables away, the woman in the wheelchair now had her back to Charli, but Charli had already seen Jack and his wife enter the restaurant and be escorted to their table. *Of all the restaurants in Savannah.*

Grayson was reading the menu as he always did, front to back, before he ordered. He mentioned going out being a nice change for them, and he even complimented Vera for her kindness. "Tell her that," Charli suggested, and Grayson smiled, "I'll let you thank her." *Those two just didn't get along.*

Charli peered over top her menu because she could not take her eyes off of Jack and Laney. She was beautiful. Her long dark hair was striking. And she was not at all frail and broken as Charli had imagined. She had broad, strong shoulders and the fitted material of her dress formed around the muscles in her back and arms. The highest boots Charli had ever seen a woman wear made her legs appear long and sexy. *Despite the wheelchair.* Her skin was like porcelain. Her features were stunning. The two of them looked like a couple. Dark hair. Dark eyes. Lean figures with some muscle. Charli felt like she was watching a movie, rooting for the beautiful couple to seek happily ever after. She certainly did want that for Jack.

Jack saw her staring, but Charli never noticed his eyes on her and Grayson as she seemed to be caught up in watching Laney. Jack understood. Laney was a woman Charli had only known about from what he had told her. To actually put a real-life image on a person who you have never seen could definitely reel you into the moment. Jack was feeling much of the same right now as he encouraged Laney to check out the menu and order whatever she wanted to try.

He stared at Grayson. His back was to him. Curly sandy brown hair. Black polo shirt and jeans. He saw his profile a time or two as he turned his head. They looked like a couple. As Charli spoke to her husband, Jack stared at her face and her eyes. She was a little too far away from his and Laney's table, but Jack already knew what those blue eyes looked like up close. She was wearing a blue denim dress, unbuttoned on her chest. He stopped himself from staring. He had to be in the moment with his wife now, who just took a generous sip of the margarita in front of her. Jack had not yet touched his.

"Try that, it's amazing. The tequila has quite a kick," Laney giggled.

"Oh boy, she's gonna get tipsy on me tonight," Jack teased, as he too took a swig of his drink. He already knew he was going to order a second one. He liked how the tequila instantly raced to his head. Seeing Charli with her husband had affected him. Grayson momentarily stepped away from the table, and it looked as if he was greeting another couple seated nearby. He stood tall and proud, like a man in charge. Jack watched him only spend a minute away from his wife at the other table. He shook hands with a gentleman and immediately returned to Charli. Charli was laughing at something he had said and Grayson appeared very animated as he spoke to her. There was a sexual energy between them that Jack instantly recognized. He noticed they too were both drinking margaritas. *Good stuff to get through an unexpected evening.*

"I'm getting this sampler platter," Laney tapped her finger on the laminated menu, and Jack leaned forward to see what she was interested in. She always had a hefty appetite. He laughed at the memory of the first time they shared a pizza when they were in junior high. Laney had eaten five pieces. She was a runner then, and her body was fit and fabulous. Jack was amazed at how her dedication to therapy had built her body up to being strong again, especially in the last year. "What are you thinking about?" Laney interrupted his thoughts.

"To eat?" he asked, snapping himself out of his thoughts of her. "I'm going with the jumbo beef enchilada smothered with queso."

"Ohhh...I'll try a bite," Laney eyes widened in delight and Jack laughed at her. Charli heard that familiar laugh from a few tables away. His eyes lit up when he looked at his wife. *They were utterly adorable together.*

Grayson and Charli ordered second margaritas by the time their combination platter of hard and soft chicken and steak tacos arrived. They also had individual plates of refried beans, rice, and corncakes.

"I'm glad I agreed to this," Charli said, glancing at her cell phone which was on the tabletop adjacent to their dinner platters.

"Then why are you looking at your phone?" Grayson teased her.

"I just need to know Liam is okay," she admitted. "Maybe I should check in with Vera, you know, just real quick?"

"No. She will text you if there is a problem," Grayson was serious.

"Vera doesn't text," Charli told him.

"Then she'll call. Stop, okay. He's fine. He's probably close to being asleep. Eat. Drink. Enjoy." Grayson bit off a huge bite of a chicken soft taco that had oozed sour cream onto his lip. He reached for his napkin, which was very much like Grayson, as there was never a moment when he was not conscientious of cleanliness. His teeth were perfect, his nose was always clean, and his face was usually shaved. Those curls on his head were the only disheveled part of him. *Sexy, too.*

"This was good for us," Charli told him, while they ate and she had actually forgotten about checking her phone for a little while.

"You're just staying that because you feel drunkie," Grayson chuckled at her.

"Maybe..." Charli responded and winked at him as she took another sip of her tequila. From across the restaurant, Jack saw her.

When only ice cubes were left in their glasses, and their plates had been cleared from the tables, all four of them were feeling relaxed and content. Their bellies were full and their heads were a little fuzzy. Charli watched Jack stand up first. This was one of those restaurants where the bill was paid at the bar. She saw him leave their table and walk toward the bar holding his ticket.

"I have Vera's gift card, I'll go pay," Charli offered, before Grayson could object. A text came through on his phone a moment ago from a client, and he started to reply when she left the table.

Charli walked up behind Jack. He was still waiting, with his ticket in hand. "Hi there," she spoke, trying to keep her voice low and her body language unreadable in case his wife glanced their way.

Jack turned to her. She was wearing booties with at least a two-inch heel. They were nearly eye to eye. "Hi Charli. I saw you and your husband from a distance."

"Me too," she stated.

"Good food here, huh?" he asked.

"Amazing." She would have said they would for sure come back, but dining out was a rare treat. "And the tequila rates over coffee," she quipped and Jack laughed.

"Yeah, I can see tipsy in those blue eyes," he chuckled under his breath, as the thirty-something Mexican man interrupted their moment from behind the register at the bar. His black glasses with a slightly visible red pinstripe around the rims caught Charli's eye. Jack paid his bill, and turned to Charli before he attempted to walk away. "I hope you have a wonderful evening with your husband. You deserve a night out."

"You too. Your wife is beautiful. She's a lucky woman." That may have been the tequila talking, providing an added boost of courage to say exactly what she was feeling, but Charli didn't care. *Laney was a beautiful woman, and a damn fortunate one.*

When Charli turned away from the bar to return to her table with Grayson, she saw Jack guiding Laney's wheelchair across the floor of the restaurant. He had bent down, from behind her, and whispered something close to her ear. Charli watched Laney's hand reach back for him and gently brush the side of his cheek.

"That's a shame, huh?" Grayson said as Charli returned to their table.

"I'm sorry? What?" Charli asked him, as he stood up from his chair to leave with her.

"That couple. I saw you watching them. She so young to be in a wheelchair. I hope it's only temporary, you know like an injury or a surgery setback."

"Regardless of her handicap, they make a striking couple," Charli offered, and she meant those words. Being different in any capacity didn't matter to her anymore. She saw past that now, thanks to her little boy.

CHAPTER 16

When Jack and Laney arrived home, he saw Richard Allison's full-size SUV parked on the driveway. It was completely solid black, even the wheels, with the darkest tinted windows Jack had ever seen on the road. The man drove around as if he ran the country. Jack rolled his eyes to himself. "Your father's here. Were you expecting him?"

"He called when you were paying the bill at the bar." Jack thought of his brief time with Charli. "I told him we were headed home."

Jack unfolded Laney's wheelchair from the back of his small pickup, and opened her door. She was ready to move into it, as she had placed her hands underneath her bottom to lift herself. "Allow me," Jack stopped her, as he picked her up and carried her in his arms. Laney momentarily wrapped her arms around his neck and their lips nearly touched.

"Tell your father not to stay long…I don't know if I can wait to get you to bed," Jack smiled as he kissed her lightly on the lips. Their desire for each other had been renewed, and Laney felt wanted and needed by him again. For so long she believed there was nothing she could give him, and she fretted she would lose him.

Jack stopped Laney's wheelchair on their front porch and stepped ahead of her to open the door. She turned the wheels herself to follow after him. All of the lights were on in their living room, and Laney's father had helped himself to a glass of scotch. That was the only reason she kept it on hand in their home. *For her father.*

"Daddy, it's good to see you." Laney was met in the middle of the living room by her father, who bent forward to kiss her on the forehead.

"Always," Richard responded, and then reached his hand out to Jack. "Jackson, thank you for taking my daughter out on the town tonight. I can see by looking at her that she had a good time. Just glowing."

Laney smiled wide. "Probably just the tequila," she laughed, and her father joined her. "That's my girl."

When Jack pulled out of the handshake with his father-in-law, Richard made full-on eye contact with him. "I hear your prototype wasn't up to par for our New York friends." First of all, they weren't Jack's friends. And he hoped none of them were Richard's either. The last thing he wanted was more help from him. And secondly, Jack was ticked. He had not told Laney anything about being rejected. Not yet anyway.

Laney's eyes widened as she looked at Jack. *He hadn't told her.*

That's why the old man was there tonight. *Damn him. He always had an agenda.* Jack willed himself to suppress his anger. "Up to par," Jack repeated Richard's word choice. "That's a gentle way to put it."

OBLIGATED

"So what is your plan B? My contact tells me you have yet to submit more, and they are willing to take a look at your other designs. Why haven't you sent them?" Ever since Jack was a thirteen-year-old boy with braces and sporadic pimples on his face, he felt the same way in the presence of this man. *Intimidated and powerless.* Jack didn't have any reason to rise above those feelings. He was equivalent to that boy still as he had nothing to show for as a man. No job. And now no designs worth a second look. Knowing that his father-in-law knew this about him crushed him a little bit more. But what was worse was the pity in Laney's eyes. She knew that he really didn't have enough talent to make it without her, which was what he had feared all along.

Jack wanted to excuse himself and bolt into the kitchen to down some of that scotch also, and he didn't even like to drink it because it tingled and burned as it lingered in his mouth.

"I'm not quite ready to send off more designs," Jack stated, vaguely.

"Don't take too long, son," Richard stated, and Jack cringed. *Don't call me son. I'm not your son.*

"Nope, I won't," Jack responded. He wanted this conversation and that man's presence in his home to be abrupt. Laney sensed how intense this was for him, so she spoke up in his defense. "I'm sure Jack will be ready when he feels like his designs are flawless. That takes time." Obviously the cowl neck poncho had not been flawless. Jack all but begged Laney to tweak it. He blamed her for the prototype's fail. That was why he never told her it was rejected. It surprised him now that she hadn't called him out in front of her father. *She always sided with her daddy.*

The drained scotch glass was on the coffee table, sans a coaster, as Jack heard the engine of Richard's SUV turnover outside on the driveway. He had said what he came for, with the implication that Jack needed to get off his ass and jumpstart his career before it went nowhere.

Laney had waited to say anything more until her father was gone. "You kept that from me," she began, and Jack never looked at her. He was seated on the edge of the sofa where he was removing his dress shoes. His feet ached from wearing those loafers. He was accustomed to sneakers. "Why?"

He looked up at her from across the room, where Laney was seated in her wheelchair. "Failure isn't something I like to brag about," he replied, noisily throwing his shoes aside on the hardwood floor.

"One submission is hardly considered not being a success. Send more, Jack. They want more, my father said so." Laney seemed adamant, and that unnerved him beyond words. He still didn't understand her refusal to help him.

"Your father said so?" Jack nearly spat the words. "Well by all means, I should listen to your father."

"Stop it, Jack. Do not mock me, or my father."

"I am not married to your father," Jack spoke harshly. "I do not care what he thinks. It's you, Laney. Take a look at the designs. Critique them. Change them. Make them ours." Jack watched her, expressionless, in her chair.

OBLIGATED

And then he quietly heard her say, "I already have."

After a pause, Jack finally spoke. "What? What does that mean? You were on my laptop and you saw my designs before? You never said anything to me. Why?"

"Because the use of my legs isn't the only thing I lost in the accident. My creativity, my eye for style and trend, and the heart I once had for the latest craze is gone. It's gone, Jack. I see great designs on the page, but that is all." Jack could hear the hopelessness in her voice, and he was stunned by her words. If that were true, this was the death of their dream.

CHAPTER 17

The following morning, Jack didn't know why but he was back, sitting inside of that empty store. He had not made any promises to Laney. He wasn't convinced he wanted this anymore. And yet, he stared at his laptop and considered sending at least one hundred designs attached to an email to New York. *What if something in there was good enough? Or, what if he designed something altogether new and different?* He thought of seeing Charli wearing the somewhat generously unbuttoned denim dress last night near the bar at the restaurant. The image of Laney's over-the-knee boots was forefront in his mind, too. A woman's style was something she owned. Laney's had grace and sentiment. Charli's was sexy and sweet, with a touch of tomboy in every piece of clothing she chose. A pair of tight denim spoke volumes in the way they rounded her ass. Jack opened a blank document on his laptop. *Today would be about designing something new.* He suddenly felt inspired by two very different women in his life. *Erase that thought. Charli wasn't exactly in his life. Was she?*

※

Vera noticed Laney was dragging on the theracycle at the start of the therapy session. "Are you alright, honey? You seem sluggish."

"I may have had too much to drink last night," she laughed. And Vera looked surprised as she explained further. "Jack and I tried the new Mexican restaurant downtown, and let me just say the margs there are ahhh-mazing."

"Oh, a little hung-over are you?" Vera giggled. She had to conceal the sudden realization on her face. *They went to the same Mexican restaurant as Charli and Grayson?* That had to be a ridiculous coincidence. And possibly an awkward one. Vera still hoped for innocence there.

"A tad," Laney smiled.

"Listen to you. You went out for dinner, I applaud you for that. You're coming along wonderfully, honey." Vera was sincere. She knew how proud Laney was of herself for conquering a fear. The idea of looking different and standing out in a crowd still bothered her.

"It was much easier than I imagined. And I made Jack happy, so it's all good."

"You would do anything for that man, wouldn't you?" Vera asked, and that comment struck Laney. *Almost anything.* She was done with designing. And Jack apparently was as well. She wanted to ask him last night what his next step would be. *Would he give up the store? Would just any nine to five job be enough for him?* She never got the chance to ask him because he came to bed after she had fallen asleep, and he was awake and out of the house before she woke up this morning. Laney worried that was purposeful because he was too disappointed in her to face her right now.

※

Jack was determined to create something new, exciting, and top of the line. He had been sitting on old, stale designs for three years. Those styles didn't excite him or thrill him. No wonder his prototype hadn't gained any immediate response. It sucked. It was drab and boring. He was inspired now, and he knew why. It was because of Charli. He would attempt to create something to drape, breathe, and react as if it were designed specifically for her body. This was inspiration from fantasy, but so be it. Jack was going with it.

※

Four hours later, Jack's sketch of the design that unfolded faster than anything he ever created before was completed. He didn't tweak it, or second guess it. He just attached it to an email, stated that it may be a little raw, and called it his prototype number two. He looked up from his makeshift desk in that empty store and for the first time in a very long time he felt accomplished. He needed to stretch his legs, breathe some fresh air. His clear view of the bus stop right now told him it was a good time.

Charli saw him walking toward her. She felt flustered and her first thought was *now was not a good time*. "Hi there," she said to him first, as she pulled up her jacket collar higher around her neck. The air was breezy and cold today.

"I saw you waiting, and I thought I would say a quick hello," Jack stated.

"I have ten minutes at the most, more like eight," Charli told him. "I don't want to seem rude or weird, but you can't be here when the bus arrives. Liam does not transition very well to me the way it is, and you would classify as a stranger."

"Of course, I understand." Jack did find it odd, the way she had to think —and live— to accommodate her son. But he admired her for it. After a pause, Jack said, "It was nice to see you out, doing something fun last night. What a great place to eat, huh?"

"Yeah, I agree," Charli meant on both accounts. "We don't do that often enough." *Or at all.*

"Us either." *Never,* Jack thought.

"I'll admit I felt a little taken aback at first," Charli initiated it. One of them needed to say it, and she knew their time to talk was limited. "Seeing you out with your wife and not being able to say hello, or mention you to Grayson, made me feel a little like what we are doing —talking now and then— is wrong."

Jack nodded. "You just said everything I was thinking. I'm not sure how I would have explained *you* if I were to introduce you to my wife. My friend, Charli? She would wonder why I hadn't mentioned you before — and when exactly had we developed a friendship. All I do is go to work and come home."

"Exactly," Charli laughed a little. "I don't think Grayson would understand friendship with the opposite sex." She wasn't sure if she understood the boundaries of it either.

"And that's where the feeling of it being wrong comes in, I think," Jack offered. "But, it's rewarding and without sounding too corny — it's therapeutic, for me to share meaningful conversation with you."

"For me, too. It makes perfect sense in my head," Charli said to him. *But not in her heart.*

"Mine also." *Then why did he just spend the last four hours sketching one of his best designs ever — from a daydream?* Jack retrieved his phone from the rear pocket of his denim. He wanted to show her the online sketch. He didn't know if he would tell her she was the inspiration behind it. But he wanted her to be the first person to see it. But then he saw the bus coming, far down the street. "I should go," he said, backing up to step off of the curb. Charli glanced down the street, and nodded her head while she attempted a half-hearted wave. It was probably best that he had not shown her the piece. It felt equivalent to betrayal to him — because Laney had always been the first to see anything he designed. But this wasn't about Laney. Not this time.

CHAPTER 18

Jack walked back to the store quickly. It was cold, and his mind was reeling. Their conversations lately had turned to the both of them trying to decipher what exactly they were doing. It wasn't wrong to have a friend and confidant outside of his marriage. It was ridiculous to feel guilty for that. What felt immoral at times were the thoughts he kept to himself about her. She was another woman. Since Jack was a thirteen-year-old boy, Laney had been the only one. He considered distance from Charli. He even thought about telling Laney he had befriended her. He omitted that idea immediately though. Laney lost a tremendous amount of self-confidence after the accident. He would never purposely hurt or destroy something she was working so hard to regain. *Just get back to work, Jack.*

When he pushed open the glass door to his store, the warm shelter from the cold felt welcoming. And then he noticed he was not alone in there. His father-in-law stood near the card table he called his desk.

"Richard," Jack nodded, as he pulled off the hood of his sweatshirt that he had worn on the walk back.

"I see you stepped out for a bit. Needed some fresh air? It's a little cold for that today," Richard spoke, as Jack stared. He was standing there in a dark suit with a matching long coat. Both the coat and the suit jacket were open to reveal a power red necktie, unable to completely cover the length of his belly bulge.

"It is cold," Jack agreed, and said no more. He shoved both his hands in the wide front pocket of his red hoodie, and he rocked back and forth on the heels of his Converse.

"I'll get right to why I'm here," his father-in-law stated. "This store is yours. I don't really care if I have to pay rent for this empty space until the end of time. I've already explained why I feel indebted to you. My daughter, my only child, loves you. You are her entire world. The deal here was obvious, or so I thought. You take care of her, and I will provide for you both."

"There never was *a deal*," Jack was sure to emphasize. "I married Laney because I love her and I want to be with her."

Richard nodded. "But then things changed. She's not exactly the woman you married."

"Don't make this about her handicap," Jack snapped at him.

OBLIGATED

"Then what should I make this about, Jack?" Richard asked him, in no uncertain terms. "Why else would you carry on with another woman? People tend to be oblivious to the fact that someone is always watching. Savannah is stocked full of people you know, people I know, or people who simply know of us."

Jack's face was expressionless. He had done nothing wrong. He and Charli and had never—

Richard walked toward him. The sound of his hard-heeled dress shoes echoed in there. He stopped close to Jack and pulled out his cell phone from his coat pocket. First, he showed Jack a photograph of him and Charli, taken through the main window of the coffeehouse, the late night they shared a table there for the first time. Second, was a shot of the two of them on the sidewalk just outside of the coffeehouse and Jack was touching Charli's cheek. *They were staring at each other like lovers.* And last, the two of them were photographed at the bus stop just minutes ago.

"Laney will never see these photos," Richard began, "and you will never see Charli Jade again. Understood?"

"I am not *seeing* her. We're friends." As Jack attempted to defend himself, he shoved away the realization of what he too had seen in that photograph outside of the coffeehouse. *They looked like they had feelings for each other. Far from platonic feelings.*

"Friends drift apart. Friends say goodbye." Richard said, before he started to walk out of the store The phone was back inside of his coat pocket, and he was buttoning up to prepare for the cold. Jack stood still in the middle of the store, but he followed him with his eyes.

"I'm not guilty of anything. I've never been unfaithful to my wife." That was the truth. Sure, his thoughts had gone there, but no one could prove that. Not even his all-knowing, all-powerful father-in-law.

"I believe you, Jack," Richard said, but his tone sounded as if he was mocking him. "Just do as I ask, and everything will be just fine."

"And if I don't?" Jack spoke up to him. He felt shaken, but he wanted to defend his own honor. "If I choose to share occasional conversation with my friend — despite your accusations and your threats — what happens then? Will you have me killed? Is that how the great Richard Allison operates?"

Richard chuckled. "I'm hardly a criminal. I'm just a wealthy man who loves his daughter. And for her sake, I would never harm you. About your lady friend though… word is money is tight for her and her husband. They have mounting bills. Loan officers make a hell of a lot more money outside of Savannah. Maybe a job transfer from our local bank would suddenly come up — far, far away from here? Maybe it already has."

When he walked out of the store, Jack just stood there. His shoulders fell as the door closed behind a man he never hated more than right now.

Charli was running late getting ready for work. It was going on six-thirty and her night shift at the hotel started at seven. She had eaten dinner with Grayson and Liam, and already gave Liam his bath. He was close to falling asleep on the sofa as Grayson pulled Charli into the kitchen. She was wearing casual clothes, denim and a sweater, and was in search of her boots when he summoned her.

"What? I'm running late," she told Grayson, as he stood there in a pair of gray sweatpants and a fitted black t-shirt. His feet were bare, as he never wore socks in their apartment.

"I wanted to bring this up at dinner, but you had your hands full with Liam. There's something huge on my mind," Grayson ran his fingers through the loose curls on his head, as Charli waited for him to go on. She honestly thought he had read something, somewhere about yet another successful innovation for Autism. And she really didn't have time for this now. "You know how my salary standstill has bothered you for years on end?"

Grayson had been making no more than thirty-seven thousand dollars annually since before Liam was born. Charli's eyes widened. "You got a raise!" she blurted out, and hoped to God it was substantial.

"Not quite," Grayson offered, "but it could happen. It's not for sure or anything, but my boss told me there's an opening for a loan officer in West Palm Beach, Florida."

Charli scoffed. "Florida? That would require moving, Gray! You know we can't move. Liam already has some of the best teachers and therapists working with him at the public school right here in Savannah, and I've been told as he advances in grade levels there, the resources for him are wonderful."

"Just listen." Grayson was the one not hearing her. "I would be making double my salary the first year, with potential to make up to one-sixteen within five years. Charli, that's some serious money for us. It's the answer to our problems."

She disagreed with that statement. Money wasn't the answer to their problems. Sure, it would help make ends meet and then some, but their struggles were not something money could make disappear. "I have to get to the hotel, Gray. I don't want to argue with you about this now. I also don't want to uproot Liam. I am not moving away from Savannah."

One year later…

CHAPTER 19

Gone was the makeshift desk in the midst of empty space inside a potential store. JACK was written on the sign out front, and clothing with only his label was sold inside. It wasn't as if he was an overnight sensation the moment his second prototype was accepted, but Jack's designs were now out there — and selling. The critics labeled Jack Horton as cutting edge in women's sportswear. He sold his label online, and only at one location — the Savannah store. It was enough for him. He wasn't on a mission to seek fame and fortune, but he had come a long way from only dreaming of success as a designer.

OBLIGATED

Jack was present in the store on most days. He still designed there — at a desk now located in an official back room, dubbed an office. He had been able to hire two sales people to assist shoppers and manage the register. The locals were huge supporters of Jack's line. He was a native of Savannah and alumni of Savannah College of Art and Design. The fact that he was seen as a local celebrity often times brought people in the door of his store just to take a look around. Jack had yet to expand to men's designs. He was still going strong with his women's sportswear line and had not needed more. He didn't want to be any busier than he already was, because his personal life demanded more of his attention now.

Sabry Allison Horton was born just five weeks ago. Her dark hair and dark eyes came from both of her parents, but her porcelain skin tone was Laney's. Jack had never known love like this. *Who knew a baby girl could become his whole world?* She and her mother.

From his desk, Jack overheard a woman ask about an item she had seen online, hoping the store had it in stock. *She wanted to wear it this weekend.* Jack laughed to himself. *Women. And the way they planned ahead.* He enjoyed designing for women, and he often thought of his initial inspiration. Sometimes a woman on the street with long blonde hair would catch his eye. But it was never her.

He regretted that there was never a goodbye. He was ashamed of the times he saw her walking outside of the window, and he made his way to the back room before she could see that he was in the store. She always gave up after several knocks on the glass. And then there was the near miss at the coffeehouse. The line was long that day when Jack walked in, and Charli was about four people ahead of him. He left without his mocha that day.

Someone was always watching, Jack remembered his father-in-law's warning. He wasn't bold enough to take the risk. The thought of jeopardizing his marriage scared him too much, so he never got the chance to say goodbye to Charli when her family moved from Savannah, Georgia to West Palm Beach, Florida. *Grayson's job transfer would be good for that family,* Jack told himself. He truly believed that Charli deserved more than the kind of life she lived in Savannah. But he missed their friendship, their mystic connection, their soul to soul talks.

※

Vera held onto Laney a little longer than she intended. Their embrace was a goodbye. This was Laney's final physical therapy session. In the last year, Vera had only been coming to the house once a week. Laney was pregnant and could not overdue her lower-body workouts. She continued to maintain and strengthen her upper body on her own time, and with Vera. Her therapy would now cease, and it was not because Laney was ready or wanted it to be over. Vera was retiring, and that too was not by choice.

OBLIGATED

"I still want to see your face often! Do you hear me?" Laney said through her tears. The baby was asleep in the nursery, but she had the monitor's receiver near her.

Vera nodded, and then paused to catch her breath. "I would like that. You know I would love to see Sabry grow." The time Vera had left to fight the battle of a progressing illness would likely not allow her the luxury of watching a child grow.

"Then let's make it happen," Laney said, placing both of her hands on the face of a woman who had become very dear to her. Vera had entered her life when it felt as if it was in ruins. She was the only one in Laney's life at that time who had been able to find an even balance between pushing her and comforting her. Laney, without a doubt, loved Vera like a mother. And since she had not had a mother in her life for nearly two decades, Laney felt crushed to be losing her. Life was unfair to everyone at some point in their lives. Vera's sudden and recent diagnosis of lung cancer had confirmed Laney's realization that life could change in an instant. This time, she understood the importance of living every day. Sabry was now her reason to do more than just exist in that chair day after day. Laney had boasted to her husband infinite times, since Sabry's birth, that she was right about bringing a baby into their world. She most definitely now had a purpose and a renewed love for life.

Vera managed to hold back the rush of tears until she was behind the wheel of her car, parked on the driveway. She sobbed to the point where it was a struggle to catch her breath. She knew for certain she could not keep her promise to Laney. Her life was soon to be stolen from her, as the doctors and the specialists forewarned that her health would fail rapidly upon diagnosis. Two weeks ago, Vera suspected she had pneumonia. She had gone to the doctor for treatment, only to discover it was cancer that consumed her lungs and it had metastasized, allowing her only a matter of weeks to live. After sixty-seven years, her time was coming to an abrupt end. And now, before she ran completely out of the time she had left, Vera wanted to see Charli one final time.

※

The waves were calmer than usual as Charli watched Liam sitting in the sand with his legs crisscrossed. He flapped his hands each time the ocean water met his bent knees first, and then reached as high as his chest. She heard him giggle, and she in turn laughed out loud. Living only walking distance from the Atlantic Ocean had turned out to be one of the greatest blessings for Charli's son. She fought the move, she resisted the change for him — and for herself. Grayson's need to be proactive and find a means to force substantial progress for Liam had finally paid off. He wanted to chase a career opportunity he probably would never again see in his lifetime, but more than that he believed water was the answer to his son's anxious and often closed-off nature. Liam by no means was cured, but he had shown significant improvement and had achieved great gains since they moved to Florida. Charli honestly believed she loved Grayson more because of it. Their bond as a family was stronger than ever.

OBLIGATED

As she counted her blessings now, she also cursed the pain and suffering that all too often crept into people's lives. She had known the devastating truth for a few days. *Vera was dying.* One phone call from four hundred miles away had sent Charli reeling. *I have to go to her*, she cried to Grayson. *She has no one else to take care of her.* He agreed. And, in just a few hours, Charli was going to be on a one-way, nighttime flight to Savannah, Georgia. Whatever time Vera had left, Charli was going to be with her. This was a woman who had seen Charli through the most devastating time in her life. It was Charli's turn to hold Vera's hand — and love her through it.

CHAPTER 20

Jack wasn't sure what time it was when he heard the baby's hunger cries from across the hallway. His eyes burned from lack of sleep and his fatigued body wasn't too eager to get out of bed, but the tiny human who had his heart was calling.

When he made his way into the pink-clad nursery, a nightlight in the wall socket allowed him to see the little legs kicking beneath the white sleeper with pink flowers. There was still room to grow in that little outfit as Jack thought she looked swallowed up in it. He cradled her the moment he saw her little scrunched up face, now rosy red from crying. "Shhh, shhh. shhh. It's all good. I'll bring you to mommy," Jack attempted to soothe her as he walked quickly across the hallway and into their bedroom. The lamp was lit near Laney's side of the bed, and she was already sitting upright, and partially topless as she was prepared to breastfeed. "Talk about at your service," Jack chuckled, and Laney reached for her baby girl. And her hunger cries ceased immediately.

Jack laid next to his girls in bed. "This is what it's all about, isn't it," he spoke with certainty. "Sometimes I feel like such a dumbass for thinking we couldn't do this, or we didn't deserve to try our hand at this."

"The dumbass surfaces in everyone from time to time," Laney teased. "All is forgiven. You did afterall play a very pertinent role in creating this little masterpiece." Laney kissed the dark hair on top of her baby girl's head.

"I love you both so much," Jack stated, wanting to savor this moment in their lives forever.

"We love you, too, daddy."

※

After her direct flight into Savannah Hilton Head International, Charli landed at nearly ten o'clock at night. She took an Uber to the old apartment building on Maue Street. Vera was expecting her, but Charli had told her not to wait up. She still had a key to Vera's place and would use it to let herself in and just go to bed. *I have not seen you in an entire year. Like hell if I am going to wait until morning to squeeze your neck.* Charli had hoped that was the case. She had missed her fiercely, too.

The number of times she walked those outside stairs, often poorly lit at night, was lost to her. But being on them again had brought back the feeling of home. Maybe it wasn't so much about those rickety stairs, or that place to live. It was because Vera was her family.

Charli turned her key in the lock, and pushed open the door. She immediately set down her suitcase and then closed and locked the apartment door behind her. The living room was well lit with two lamps, one on each end of Vera's maroon suede sofa, and the television's volume was almost too low to hear. Asleep in her favorite recliner chair, with an ugly green afghan tucked around her body, was Vera.

Charli stopped and stared. She had an oxygen mask placed on her lap, upside down like a turtle shell. Charli supposed it was within reach for a just-in-case scenario. She had naively hoped Vera's lungs were not failing her that quickly. She selfishly wanted more time with her.

She sat down on the end of the sofa closest to Vera's recliner. She slipped off her ballet flats. She had worn crop denim and a white v-neck t-shirt, forgetting that it would be chillier in Savannah. Her sun-kissed skin now had chill bumps. Charli looked to the opposite end of the sofa and reached for an ivory fleece blanket folded there. She covered herself and curled up on for a little sleep before Vera would be awake.

OBLIGATED

The living room was bright from the sun peering through the window blinds that were now wide open. When Charli fluttered her eyelids, she caught a glimpse of Vera standing over her.

"It's just like you not to listen. I clearly instructed you to wake me when you arrived last night," Vera wagged a finger at her, but her facial expression revealed how happy she really was to see her again.

Charli sat up quickly. She could feel the sleep in her eyes, and assumed her mascara had given her a rough night appearance. But she didn't care. *She was home.* For a moment, when Vera embraced her, Charli thought she felt as strong as ever. But then she could hear the wheezing coming from her chest. Charli loosened her grip. She was afraid she might squeeze her too tight. "I've missed you so much," Charli heard herself say, as her voice caught in her throat.

"Not nearly as much as I ached for your presence in my life," Vera confessed. If this was it, if she was that close to the end of her days, there was going to be no holding back on her part. "Those stairs outside of my window haven't looked the same since the day you left. I had no reason to peer out, and rest my elbows on the sill. Don't get me wrong, I know the move was the best thing for your boy and your family. I am not that selfish. But now that you're here, I just don't plan to let you go for awhile."

Charli smiled, and gripped her hand. "Same here." She didn't plan to let her go so easily either.

Vera was as self-sufficient as Charli expected. She was able to bathe and dress herself. She did sit down at the kitchen table for rest afterwards, and Charli offered to scramble a few eggs while Vera said she could handle the buttered toast.

After breakfast, Vera settled into her recliner to *rest her eyes.* And that's when Charli slipped into a pair of sneakers she had packed. She was now dressed in black leggings and a white half-zip Sherpa pullover. The zipper track on it was gray and the sleeve cuffs matched. It felt cozy as she stepped out onto the stairs after she locked the door behind her to Vera's apartment. She would just take a short walk, that familiar path, to the coffeehouse.

When Charli rounded the corner downtown, she saw the sign. The Uber driver had not taken the downtown route last night to get to the apartment building, so this was Charli's first chance to see for herself and in person how JACK's name, his brand, his dream to have a label, was now up in lights. She felt a sense of pride for him, the man who had come to mean something special to her in a short amount of time. *Instantly*, if she was honest with herself.

She saw the OPEN sign in the window. For now, she would forget her hankering to have a vanilla latte from that coffeehouse across the street. In Florida, she still had not found a place as tasty.

OBLIGATED

The door chimed when she stepped inside. The empty space she once remembered, from merely one year ago, was transformed into racks upon racks of clothing, along with several rounded sections of wooden shelves with folded clothing items — much like the Sherpa she was wearing. Charli had heard of Jack's success after they moved from Savannah, and she was certain she was one of the first to order a JACK piece online. Now, she had several.

A middle-aged woman greeted her from across the store. Charli's response was friendly, as she wondered how she would ask if Jack Horton was around. *Had he ever stopped in, or was he too big of a name now for petty things like that?* Charli smiled to herself. The Jack she knew would never let success consume him.

Charli had three items draped over her arm. The JACK sportswear line called her name every time. Shopping was never on her radar when she lived in Savannah, but now Grayson's job had allowed her that luxury. She knew she needed to pay for her items, grab a latte across the street, and then get back to Vera.

When Charli was at the register, she told herself she had nothing to lose. *Just ask.* "This line is my new obsession," she teased, and the woman laughed out loud. "So, is the designer still local?"

"Oh yes, Jack lives and works here still." *Here? As in this store?*

"I'm sure his buyers love to run into him," Charli stated. *I knew him when…*

"Yes, like you, many women ask if he's here when they're shopping. He'll be popping in soon. His morning hours are getting later and later since he and his wife had a baby."

Charli felt her eyes widen. *Oh my gosh. A baby? Jack had a baby! Laney had gotten her wish. Life was incredibly good… sometimes.* "That's wonderful!" Charli reacted with probably too much excitement for a stranger, or just a fan.

"It is wonderful. Given all that the two of them have had to face in their young lives, it's a real blessing."

Charli nodded. *It certainly was.* As the saleswoman handed her the bag, with the receipt for her purchases inside, Charli wasn't ready to end this conversation. She wanted to know more. *Boy or girl? What's the name? I'm sure the baby is beautiful, coming from two gorgeous parents.* Charli thanked her and walked out of the store.

Jack parked along the street, and began to walk up the sidewalk to his store. The feeling of walking in there every day was something he would never take for granted. That once empty space was now a store where on most days the door was revolving. The fact that people, women for themselves and men for their girlfriends and wives, wanted to buy his line was a constant inspiration for him.

He carried his laptop, tucked underneath his arm. Jack still appeared to live simply. He wore khakis or denim daily, and always with Converse. When he was just a few steps from the door, he saw it open. He stopped to politely wait for the patron. Charli stepped out of the door, turned her head, and looked directly at him. "Jack…" He looked good. Different in some aspects. His hair was a little longer, his face donned overnight scruff.

"Charli!" She looked beautiful. Different to him though. Her once long blonde hair was shorter, now two or three inches above the shoulders. Her blue eyes were still bright. She looked healthier, perhaps more well-rested. Those twelve-hour all-night shifts were never good for anyone.

She reached for him, and he opened his arms. They met in an obviously unplanned, impromptu embrace. It was close, tight gripped, friendly, and meaningful. And simultaneously, they both realized they had never held onto each other before. Never hugged. Hardly touched. This felt long overdue for both of them. Charli pulled back first, but she didn't want to.

"What are you doing here?" were Jack's first words.

She smiled, and lifted up her full bag of purchases. "Shopping at my favorite store."

Jack's smile grew wider. She knew. And he had already spotted her wearing his Sherpa half-zip pullover. That was an online only item. *Orders were being sent to West Palm Beach.* Jack's heart swelled.

"It's amazing, isn't it? I don't mean to blare my own horn, but geez people are buying my designs! The sportswear line has been a huge hit."

"It's all I wear," Charli stated as if it was a matter of fact.

"Thank you," Jack placed his hand over his heart. "You should be getting the friends and family discount." He was teasing, but actually wanted to make something like that happen.

"To say I knew you when is such a thrill for me," Charli boasted.

Jack laughed. "I can see the move was good for you, I hope the same for your boy, your family."

"I fought that change, I really did. But, yes, it was a blessing in disguise. Liam loves the water and we are a less than a minute walk from the ocean." Jack could see her sun-kissed face and neck. She looked beautiful with a little color. "I never had the chance to tell you, to say goodbye. I'm sorry, Jack. I've regretted that more than you know."

Jack looked down at his feet. He could have allowed her to say goodbye. He was just too much of a coward. "It's okay. I was sad to see you go, but I hoped for only better things for you — and your family." They could have stood there and talked forever. It was that effortless between them again.

"Speaking of family, I just heard inside... you have a baby!" Charli didn't contain her excitement this time.

Jack chuckled and nodded his head multiple times. "She's amazing, she's beautiful, she's the tiniest thing ever, and I love her with my entire being. I can't tell you how good it feels to be a daddy. Her daddy." Jack was gushing, and Charli smiled so big. That's all she had been doing for minutes with him. So much so that her face hurt.

"A little girl," Charli sighed, loving this for him. "What's her name?"

"Sabry Allison," Jack spoke. "Allison was my wife's maiden name."

Charli nodded. "Beautiful."

As cars drove by on the cobblestone street near the curb where they stood and peopled walked by them, Jack pulled out his cell phone from the rear pocket of his khakis. He turned the screen toward Charli.

"She's the most beautiful baby girl I've ever seen," Charli fed the new daddy's biased opinion, but she wholeheartedly agreed.

"Thank you. We think so, too," he referred to his wife.

"How's Laney? Was the pregnancy okay for her?" Charli had hoped Jack's fears were unfounded. Especially the ones he had for once the baby arrived and needed both her mother and father to care for her.

"It was damn near perfect. She was right. A baby gave her a purpose. My life right now is so good it scares me. I don't want anything to take this joy away." Jack's smile fell.

"Live for the moment, my friend," Charli stated, as she reached out to squeeze his hand. He smiled. He felt it, too.

"I feel like I have a million more questions for you. Why are you back, for one?" Jack asked.

This time Charli's face fell. "A friend, a dear friend and once a neighbor at the old apartment building needs me. She doesn't have long to live." Charli felt her eyes well up with tears, and Jack immediately spoke.

"I'm sorry. My God, that's awful."

"It is. She's sixty-seven and has been forced to retire. She was still helping people. She's one of the best therapists I've ever come across, and with Liam I've met my share in the last four years."

"Therapist?" Jack knew. He immediately placed Vera Faye. She was, afterall, Laney's godsend of a physical therapist following the accident. He had no idea though that she too lived in that same apartment building. "She was Laney's PT for years. This is tearing her apart, too. She loves Vera Faye like a mother."

"What an incredibly small world," Charli replied. *She's like a mother to me, too.*

"Hug her for us. Tell her we are thinking about her, and if there is anything she needs…anything, please ask," Jack offered. "I know people say that, but I truly mean it."

Charli nodded. "I know you do."

Jack wanted to ask her how long she was staying in Savannah. He was close to suggesting that they have coffee, just right across the street at their old stomping ground, sometime soon. *For old time's sake. For the sake of never saying goodbye, for the purpose of now being given the chance to catch up.*

"I should go. I know you have to get to work," she said.

"And you need to get back to Vera," Jack added.

"See you soon?" Charli hoped.

"You know where to find me. And don't you dare leave Savannah without saying goodbye this time." This time, Jack wouldn't allow himself to be fearful, and heartless. He wouldn't avoid her. He wouldn't allow himself to feel guilt or shame. Charli was his friend.

CHAPTER 21

Charli made her way across the street for a vanilla latte before she walked back to the apartment building. She had not planned to be gone that long, and she hoped Vera was still resting. *If not, would she tell her there was a long line at the coffeehouse?* She did have her shopping bag from JACK with her. *Maybe Charli would finally confide in Vera about what Jack Horton once meant to her?* And still did.

She used her key to quietly turn the lock. When she stepped inside, she found Vera upright in her recliner, taking a few breaths from the oxygen mask before she set it back on her lap. Charli had yet to see her with it strapped on her face. Maybe it was a vanity thing, or perhaps there wasn't a constant need for it yet? The two of them had a lot of talking to do. And Charli's one wish right now was for them to have all the time in the world together.

"I would have bet money on where you were!" Vera slapped her leg and howled with laughter. That laugh sounded weaker than Charli remembered, but her mannerisms remained the same. *Oh how Charli had missed her.*

Charli raised her cup to Vera and smiled. They both ignored the shopping bag in her other hand. "I should have brought you something, I'm sorry, I assumed you would still be asleep."

"No need. I've never really been into coffee, just here and there in my life. My ex-husband drank it like water though." Charli momentarily wondered if Vera would begin to spend her time thinking about her life, those she loved, and those she lost. It was a natural process to rehash it all before closing the book on the one and only chance to live a fulfilling life. Charli knew Vera, like everyone else, had regrets.

"How long has it been since you've seen him, your ex-husband I mean," Charli clarified her question.

"It's not that I'd never seen him after we divorced. He was a police officer in this city. A few times he caught me speeding through downtown, but his lights never went on, he never pulled me over. Guess he already knew what a handful I was!" More howled laughter, followed by an intense cough this time. Charli laughed, but she wanted to tell Vera to take it easy a little bit. "He had a family with his new, younger wife. Two children, both sons. It took me awhile to get over the hurt from that one. Saul always told me he never wanted children. Guess his new little lady was able to change his mind."

"Do you regret not having your own children?" Charli asked, as she sat down on the end of the sofa to be closer to her.

"I do, of course yes I do," Vera admitted. "But then, my path has merged with some very special people in my life who I could not love any more if they were my own." Charli smiled. She knew Vera was also referring to Jack's wife.

"I did a little shopping while I stepped out," Charli said, acknowledging the bag now on the floor at her feet.

"That store is really something, I hear," Vera began. "The man behind the designs, Jack Horton, is the husband of one of my former patients. Good people."

She and Vera had never made that connection before, but that wasn't surprising given the fact that in Vera's profession she was bound by an oath to respect the privacy of her patients.

"I knew Jack before he was famous," Charli admitted, the first time to anyone. And it felt good to say it. Vera flashed back to the time she saw the two of them together on the sidewalk in front of the coffeehouse, late one night. To any onlooker, they would have appeared to be smitten lovers. "We just always seemed to bump into each other, at the coffeehouse and on the street. I mean, I lived in this apartment building and his store was just cattycornered from here." None of that meant they were bound to connect on the same crossed path. But they had.

"I also knew him before he found success," Vera stated. "He's a dedicated husband. I'm sure you know he married young, only to have such tragedy occur."

"I can't imagine being confined to a wheelchair at any age, but her life was just beginning," Charli shook her head. Something that happened more than four years ago disturbed her. It was so permanent. And terribly sad. Anyone would feel that way, but Charli especially did because she witnessed Jack's pain from it still a few years later.

"But her life was not over," Vera chimed in, adamantly. "She, like someone else I know, just had to alter expectations in order to find happiness and contentment."

Charli smiled, and reached to squeeze Vera's knee. "That will always be the best advice anyone has ever given me."

"So tell me, did you run into your friend, Jack on your quick shopping excursion?" The way that Vera had said *your friend* sounded a little emphasized to Charli, but she let it go.

"I did, actually, just as I was leaving. What a nice pleasant surprise! He has a brand new baby girl! His label has found the success it deserves. Life is good for him." Vera refrained from pointing out to Charli that her face lit up when she spoke of *her friend*.

"From what you've told me, and judging by how wonderful you look, I assume life is equally as good in West Palm Beach for you, honey?"

"It is. Liam has done so well with the change. I've said this before, but that massive body of water made a significant difference in his world. He's still Liam, quirky, fit-filled, and delayed in so many areas for a four-year-old, but he's just happier and more content with the world around him." It felt hard to believe for Charli to relay such positive news to Vera. For so many years, she spoke her worst fears and overwhelming worries to this woman who listened like no other.

"They do claim everything happens for a reason," Vera quoted the old cliché, but selfishly wondered why she had only been allocated sixty-seven years of life, and would be robbed of the chance to enjoy her retirement. She questioned, especially so much of what she witnessed in her profession, why there was helplessness and pain in the world. She did know that many times in life the things that led to awakening and compassion, and even forgiveness, often could not be attained without going through something terrible first. It was life. The good. The bad. The suffering. The rewards.

"I agree," Charli spoke, but she also had her share of doubts and unanswered questions. She was staring down an impossible obstacle right now as she definitely wasn't ready to face losing Vera.

"So tell me something," Vera began, "how long do I have you for?" Charli had never mentioned a scheduled return flight to West Palm Beach.

"For as long as you need me," Charli replied in what was barely a whisper, because this time she tried unsuccessfully to choke back the tears.

CHAPTER 22

Jack practically bounced through the door at the end of the day. He never could stand to be away from his baby girl for too long. Laney felt such joy every time she heard him express that. Sabry was their baby. She had brought them closer together, and sealed them as a unit, a family. If Laney ever had her doubts about losing Jack following the accident, those were gone the moment she knew she was carrying Jack's child. He was a man of honor, loyalty, and commitment, she was certain of that.

He found the two of them in the nursery, where Laney sat in her wheelchair, holding a sleeping Sabry. "I was just about to put her down," Laney kept her voice low. "She fell asleep while I was nursing, so this little catnap won't last long before she's hungry again."

Jack suppressed a chuckle. The two of them, his girls, most definitely made coming home at the end of the day something he looked forward to. "So it's going okay without any help here during the day while I'm gone?" Jack asked, scooping up the baby from his wife's arms. His intention was to put her in her crib, which was just a few feet from where he stood, but holding her was too enticing so he stood in place and swayed his body in a rocking motion.

"It is," Laney responded, in reference to Jack's suggestion that they hire a part-time nurse to give Laney some assistance and the occasional break. "You know what I wish for though... a way Vera could be with me a portion of the day." They both knew that was not possible, as she was ailing and would decline quickly according to the doctors and specialists.

"She would have been perfect for the job," Jack agreed, as he contemplated telling Laney about Charli and her connection to Vera. "I was actually talking to a customer at the store today about Vera. It was one of those small-world realizations. She used to live in the same apartment building as Vera, but moved to Florida. Vera's declining health brought her back here, um, I guess until the end." Jack cleared his throat. He should not have felt nervous speaking to Laney about Charli, but he was.

"Oh my," Laney sadly reacted. "How in the world did you stumble on that subject with a stranger?" This was exactly why Jack should not have brought up Charli. He never had to lie to Laney before, and he didn't want to start now.

"Oh you would be surprised the things my customers bring up in conversation, they like to tell me their life stories while they shop. I'm not usually out in the store that often, but when I am someone always seems to trap me." Jack chuckled a bit.

"There are just bunch of star-struck women out there," Laney teased. "Should I be jealous?"

Jack rolled his eyes. "Yeah I'm hit on daily."

"So this woman, she's obviously close to Vera. I wish you would run into her again," Laney stated.

"What?" Jack asked. "Why?"

"Because you could tell her to give Vera a hug from me. Just so she would know that I'm thinking about her."

Jack nodded. "I actually did tell her exactly that," Jack admitted. "I explained our connection to Vera, and how beneficial and special she was to you for years."

"That was kind of you, honey, thank you," Laney blew him a kiss from the two fingers she had pressed to her lips.

When Sabry stirred in his arms, Jack focused his attention on her as she opened her big brown eyes and stared up at him. "Hey baby girl, your daddy's home. I missed you so much. I think you got bigger, yes I do, I think you grew since this morning…"

Laney watched Jack closely. She listened, and smiled. Her heart was full. *She was the luckiest woman in the world.*

<hr />

The decline in Vera's health was unreal. Charli was taken aback when Vera told her she hired hospice to guide her through the remaining days. That seemed so final to Charli, and the sadness in her eyes was evident to Vera.

"It's alright, honey. They will come and go to help me manage my pain. I told them I had someone staying with me who I want to savor my time alone with."

"You did?" Charli teared up so easily since her arrival to Savannah. It tore her apart inside to watch Vera face the end of her life. "You know I'm not going anywhere. I'm here for whatever you need." Vera now had the oxygen mask strapped to her face consistently as she reclined back in her favorite chair. It sometimes got in the way of her large black, wire-rimmed glasses.

Charli had just taken instructions from the hospice nurse, who said he would return first thing in the morning. Charli must have seemed overwhelmed, because the male nurse reminded her that she had his number and should not hesitate to call with any questions or concerns.

When she closed the door behind him, she noticed Vera was asleep again. Her pain had been greater than she let on. The

OBLIGATED

hospice nurse revealed that truth to Charli.

She was going to clean up the kitchen and keep up with things around the apartment and in the laundry room while Vera was resting, but a second knock at the door almost immediately following the exit of the hospice nurse had her wondering if he returned.

Charli opened the door and found a man, probably close to seventy, on the other side. "Hi," he spoke first. "I'm Saul Faye. I used to be married to Vera."

Charli didn't know if she should invite him inside. It wasn't her place to make that decision. She looked back, behind her, to find Vera's eyes still closed. She was lost in some serious slumber. "She's asleep, but please come in," Charli stepped back for him to enter. He was only about an inch taller than Charli, which would make him under six foot. His thinning hair was completely white, and his belly was round beneath is untucked plaid shirt. She watched him stand in place, just over the threshold, and he stared. Charli wondered what his thoughts were. *Did he too have regrets?*

"Hard to believe," he said, softly, and Charli watched his eyes turn watery.

"It is. I'm having a difficult time grasping all of this," she admitted. "I'm Charli Jade, Vera's friend. I actually used to be her neighbor, one floor up."

Saul reached for Charli's hand. "Nice to meet you. Thank you. It's comforting to know that she has someone who cares so much. I am sure at a time like this, Vera must wish she had had children."

"Probably," Charli agreed. "Would you like something to drink? Or to sit down?"

"He likes his coffee black, and he's a man who prefers to stand when he's somewhere he doesn't totally feel comfortable." Vera's voice sounded strong, coming from across the room, in the recliner chair.

Charli spun her head around toward Vera, and then she turned back to Saul. The smile on his face immediately put her at ease. She was definitely in the presence of two people who once shared something. At least their love and their time spent married to each other had been special enough to have brought this man back to say goodbye.

"Actually, I will sit down because I do feel comfortable in your presence, my dear," Saul spoke with straightforwardness and an evident twinkle in his eye, as Charli giggled because she could have sworn Vera's full cheeks looked slightly flushed.

"I need to clean up in the kitchen," Charli spoke up and exited the room. She didn't think either one of them heard her or noticed her walk away.

Vera's apartment wasn't very spacious. It was even smaller than the one Charli and Grayson had crammed everything they owned into with Liam. Being in the kitchen, just around the corner, didn't prevent Charli from overhearing the conversation in the adjacent room.

"Funny how it takes being at death's door to bring someone back to say hello... or in your case, goodbye," Vera's tone was colder now. She may have caused pain to this man, but she had suffered too.

OBLIGATED

"I'm not here for selfish reasons like that," Saul told her. "I don't need a goodbye to feel closure or better satisfied with myself. This is about you and I, and the life we shared. No, it didn't end well…but I loved you and I know you loved me."

"I never doubted the kind of man you were, and still are Saul," Vera paid him a sincere compliment. I know you have no regrets, but I sure as hell do."

Charli had not moved a muscle in the kitchen. She listened, but she had not seen Saul kneel down in front of the recliner, one slow landing at a time on each knobby knee cap, and he reach for Vera's hand. "Don't speak for me. I most certainly do have regrets. Even after all these years, I still wish I had been man enough to forgive."

Vera could not conceal the surprise she felt, or the tears that broke free from behind her glasses and trickled around her oxygen mask. "Leave it to you to woo a woman on her deathbed, Saul Faye. Thank you. I've hated what I did for most of my life. The last thing in this world I ever wanted to do was hurt the man I loved more than anything. I just lost sight of that for awhile."

"Shush already. No sense in rehashing anything," Saul spoke. "Just listen to me, listen closely to what I have to say before both of my knees give out from underneath me." Charli heard Vera attempt her legendary howl, but it was muffled from behind her oxygen mask. And a weak cough erupted. "My damaged pride got in the way. I sulked for years about something that was over and done with. I married again, I became a father. I would not trade my children and those memories for anything. I have grandchildren now," Vera watched him smile, obviously boasting with pride. "What I have wished for, many times, was a redo. With you. You should have been the mother of my children. That is my biggest regret of my seventy-years. So don't think you're the only one with lament. You're not that special." Vera smiled at him. Most of all, she may have missed the way he teased her. It was always with love. And still was.

Saul left her with a gentle kiss on the cheek, and a soft whisper in her ear that Vera was certain she would never forget in her final days. "Take care, Mrs. Faye."

CHAPTER 23

Even though Charli heard everything from the kitchen and had tears rolling down her cheeks in response, Vera reiterated word for word what she and Saul had spoken to each other.

"Oh honey, if you've learned anything from me in the years we've known each other, I hope it's to think twice before you do something that even remotely has the potential to change your life. Or, as in my case, ruin it."

"Why did you do it? I mean I feel like I know you well. Why did you choose to be with another man?" Charli distinctly recalled Vera saying she had lost sight of what her husband truly meant to her. They had drifted apart some. And then a male friend and confidant had been there for her." Charli thought of Jack. And of how much she loved Grayson, and the family they shared with Liam.

"That's the thing, the part I really and truly cannot explain to myself after all these years. I was captivated by something almost out of my control. To be able to escape real life, and valid problems. It was as if I had found a new identity, aside from being the wife of Officer Faye, aside from being a renowned therapist in Savannah. I'm not even sure if the man I called my friend, the man I came onto, would have ever initiated anything more between us. We were attracted to each other, we both confessed to that, but we should have respected those boundary lines." Again, a part of Vera felt as if she was preaching to Charli.

"I understand," Charli did not hesitate to admit. "Maybe more than you know." Vera waited for Charli to continue. "I can't explain this, even to myself, but I'm going to speak it to you. A little over a year ago, before we moved from here, I met Jack Horton, the wanna-be designer then. I've told you how our paths crossed often. It just seemed like we were destined to have these heart-to-heart conversations whenever we met. We sympathized with each other's hardships. I'm telling you, Vera, no one gets the crap that life hurdles at us unless they've been through something. He felt obligated to his wife, as I have many times to my son. We connected on a deeper level that I really cannot explain. Was it sexual? No, not in the true actual act-on-it sense. We've never been intimate, but I cannot say we don't feel the sparks of intimacy when we are together. We do respect each other's marriages and families. Jack has a child now."

Vera continued to listen raptly. She never wanted to allow herself to believe Charli had cheated on her husband. But again, she had seen her with Jack Horton. "How did you feel when you saw him again, after an entire year away?" Vera asked her.

"Like no time had passed," Charli stated. "Even though our lives have changed and gone on for the better for both of us, that connection remains. It's such a comfort, but it doesn't put me completely at ease. It's too exciting for that." Charli realized she was admitting that fact to herself for the first time ever right at this moment.

"That kind of thrilling emotion only means trouble. Promise a dying woman something. If your paths cross again, focus on your family and think of Jack's wife and child. You have the power to protect people from getting hurt, yourself included." Charli watched Vera momentarily close her eyes. She needed rest, and Charli wished to stop thinking — and confessing to something that was never going to be anything but thoughts and perhaps feelings she had already spent entirely too much time analyzing. Being back in Savannah had stirred it too much.

※

A week went by. Charli avoided the store, and when she made quick trips for a latte at the coffeehouse, she always stayed on the opposite side of the street. She missed Liam and Grayson, and their home near the beach. Her days with Vera had now become long, as she slept most of the time. It was painful to watch, and draining to care for her around the clock. The male hospice nurse was completely aware of that, so he often sent Charli out for some air, or for something better to eat than what she had been making herself at the apartment.

She sat by Vera now, alongside of the hospital bed that was brought in to make her more comfortable. It's what the hospice nurse said everyone does *near the end*. Charli had cried so much in the last week, she believed she was out of tears. She also had told Vera goodbye and expressed her love and gratitude for her an infinite number of times. She wanted to say it repetitively. She wanted her to know how loved and appreciated she was in this life before she closed her eyes for the final time.

It had been sixteen hours since Charli had last seen Vera awake. This was the comatose state the nurse had prepared her for. Charli was so tired. She slumped over the bed, dropped her head, and only closed her eyes to rest for a moment when she felt Vera's hand on top of hers. "It's time," her voice was raspy and her words were drawn out. "I'm going to go now." Charli wanted to protest. *No! This wasn't fair. She need one more day with her.* But this wasn't about her. This was the end of Vera's suffering. She had to let her go peacefully.

"I love you, Vera. I love you so much." She wanted to tell her some ridiculous things like — to be happy in the hereafter, to be safe in her travels there, but really it was all beyond anyone's control. It happened in an instant. Vera's eyelids dropped, and Charli simply trusted she would cross over to the other side. No one was more deserving of those angel wings.

OBLIGATED

For the longest time, Charli sat bent over Vera's now lifeless body. She couldn't let go, nor she could she stop crying. But she had felt so privileged to be the one person beside this amazing woman when she took her last breath.

CHAPTER 24

Charli was probably too distraught to leave the apartment building, but she had to. The coroner had arrived to take Vera. Her body was going to be transported to the university for study, and her organs would be donated. It was exactly like Vera to want to help others long after she was gone. Vera requested no memorial service, and she had bequeathed everything she owned to Charli, which included her retirement fund. Charli cried when she read her will, in the sealed manila envelope on the kitchen counter. Vera had asked her to open it after she was gone.

OBLIGATED

She called Grayson with the sad news that Vera was gone, and he gave her a sympathetic listening ear on the opposite end of the phone. They agreed that she would just close up the apartment, and they would continue to pay rent on it, until they were able to move Vera's things out of it. Some things they would donate, and others Charli would keep forever. Before Charli ended their call, she expressed to Grayson how much she loved and missed him and Liam. In just a couple days, she would be home with them again.

She had nowhere else to go. Just the coffeehouse, she thought, as she made her way along the cobblestone streets. Jack was going to go home for lunch, and he was about to pull his vehicle away from the curb when he saw Charli. He immediately felt alarmed, and she appeared to stagger down the street. She wasn't using the sidewalk. She was walking along the curb on those uneven cobblestones.

Jack got out of his vehicle and shut the door quickly behind him. "Hey! Charli!" he called out to her. She never looked. It was as if she was in her own separate world, oblivious to the happenings all around her. Jack weaved in and out of the passing cars and ran to her. He grabbed her by the arm and brought her to what he believed was safety on the sidewalk. This ironically reminded him of the first time he attempted to rescue her alongside of the road when she had a near miss with a car as she stepped off of the curb at her son's bus stop. "Charli…"

She jumped from his grip on her upper arm. "It's okay, it's me, Jack. What happened?" Jack watched her face fall. The tears formed in her eyes and she began to sob. He pulled her close on the sidewalk directly in front of the coffeehouse. They had stood there together once before. She clung to him. Jack ignored the stares from the passerby. He just held her tighter when he heard her say that Vera had died today.

"I'm sorry, oh dammit I fell apart. Could we be anymore public right now?" Jack tried not to chuckle at her words as Charli eventually pulled out of his arms. Her blonde hair was tucked behind both ears and she was wearing a pink baseball cap on her head. Her mascara had left stains under her eyes.

"Don't apologize. You've had a rough visit back here, and today's pain just got the best of you, that's all."

Charli attempted a smile as she wiped the remaining tears from her face with the back of her hands. "Thanks for being here. I just had to leave that apartment, and the coffeehouse seemed like a good escape."

"Let's go in," he said, motioning toward the door. "We'll each have a cup. You need to sit down for awhile to regroup." Charli hesitated to agree. She was most vulnerable now and definitely able to recognize that. She also could hear Vera's warning echoing inside of her head.

"I don't know if we should," she heard herself say.

"Charli, you have only what, one or two more days left here in Savannah? It'll be a goodbye treat, on me." Jack did not appear to see any risk in what he was proposing. Charli believed she could have been overreacting. She chided herself for it, and then nodded her head in answer. Jack then held the door for her as they walked into the coffeehouse together.

OBLIGATED

After their first sips in silence, Charli spoke first. "She left everything to me." Jack of course knew she was referring to Vera. "Her material things, her retirement fund."

"That's incredible. So she had no family, or kids of her own?" Jack had never inquired about Vera to Laney before. He wasn't even sure how much Laney was aware of in regards to her therapist's personal life.

"She had an ex-husband, but no children. So many people loved her though, like you told me Laney did. Her patients grew really attached to her. She just had that kind of persona." Charli needed to talk about the friend she lost, and Jack allowed her to say whatever she was thinking and feeling in her raw state of grief.

"The last name, Faye isn't all that common around here," Jack stated, to make conversation. "Other than a city police officer for a lot of years when I was a kid, I don't know of any other Fayes."

"That's Saul Faye you're referring to," Charli told him. "I just met him last week actually. He was Vera's husband for almost twenty years."

"Ah, again, small world," Jack nodded. "So why did they divorce? Did Vera ever say?" This was the question Charli had not wanted to come up. *Had she the right to share such private information? Did she really want to discuss with Jack the chain reaction from having an extramarital affair?*

"An affair," she spoke, hesitantly, "and then Saul eventually remarried and had children with his new wife."

"Ouch," Jack said. "Sounds like another story that confirms everyone goes through their fair share of pain and suffering. That's unfortunate that Vera was treated so badly. I'm sure her husband's affair and then remarriage and births of babies with his once-upon-a-time mistress had really burned her."

Charli again hesitated. *Should she set him straight, or just leave it at that? Did it really matter after almost three decades later?* "It wasn't Saul who had the affair," Charli said right before she momentarily looked down at her coffee.

"Oh," Jack responded, obviously surprised. "I suppose everyone has secrets, too."

"But is that really okay?" Charli piped up, almost unnerved by how Jack just shrugged off the fact that Vera had an affair that consequently ruined her marriage. "No matter how tempting it is, there are boundaries to respect, aren't there?"

Jack's eyes widened. "Absolutely. Are you okay?" he recognized what he thought was annoyance in her voice and body language.

"Yes, sorry. I'm just venting. I'm sad and I'm angry."

"You're grieving," Jack told her, as they both now stared at the bottoms of their empty coffee cups.

There were confusing, pent up feelings between them. And questions they wanted to seek answers to, but both knew they couldn't or shouldn't attempt to go there. A moment later,

OBLIGATED

Charli regretfully stood up and said she had to leave. And Jack let her walk out of the coffeehouse, after he uttered that he understood.

CHAPTER 25

Charli arrived at Savannah Hilton Head International. Her flight back to West Palm Beach was scheduled for departure in one hour. She had already checked in two suitcases. One, was her own. And the other was of one Vera's in which she had packed some sentimental things of hers to bring home. Charli wondered if losing Vera would ever hurt any less. She sat alone and teary-eyed in a section of the airport that wasn't swarming with travelers at the moment.

Lost in thought, and looking down at the floor at her feet, a pair of black Converse shoes appeared close to her. Charli dashed her head upright. "Jack? What are you doing here?" She had made absolutely no attempt to run to him in the last couple of days. It was time to return to her life and her family who needed her six hours away from where their home used to be. Charli had been afraid to face Jack again. And she couldn't bring herself to say goodbye. She had enough of that final farewell feeling lately to last a lifetime.

"I think it's obvious," Jack stated. "You never said goodbye."

Charli looked down at her feet, and his, again.

"What time does your flight leave?" he asked her.

"In one hour," she replied, looking back up at him.

"Come with me."

"Jack, I'm going home today."

"It's just outside. Step out for some fresh air, and a little privacy. I'll have you back in here in time to board." Jack seemed confident, while Charli still felt skeptical. But she followed him regardless.

She walked with him, considerably far out and near the border of the parking lot, which was almost too close to the runway. "I used to come out here when I was a kid, brand new to the driving world. I watched the planes take off from the hood of my car." He sat down on the hood of his little red pickup truck now. Even after success, he still drove that old beater. "You've avoided me. You wanted to fly out of here and never look back. I want us to talk about why."

Charli stayed silent, as Jack continued. "I get it. I did the same thing to you a year ago." This puzzled Charli. "I was in my store those times when you knocked on the window, those taps got louder with each one, before you left. I gave up mochas for a week, believing I had decreased my chances of bumping into you at the coffeehouse. I was afraid to say goodbye to you. I was scared to death of what I might say, or do, to try to change your mind. That's just it though. I knew I had no right to change your plans, because I had an obligation to my wife — just as you had to Grayson and your son. Nothing has changed really. I have a family now, too. I have more obligations. It's good, it's perfect. And yet, I'm here."

"Why am I here?" Jack asked her, as if he was on mission to continue speaking until she listened and truly heard him. "Because it's time to talk about it." Charli felt her heartbeat quicken. Nothing good was going to come of speaking a truth they couldn't embrace with all they were as human beings.

"My father-in-law is someone I probably haven't discussed too much with you. He's a man of power and wealth. He throws his money around to get what he wants. He loves his only daughter, my wife, fiercely. And now he's trying to have the same kind of hold on his granddaughter. He claims it's love. He saw you and I together, here and there, in downtown Savannah. He had photographs taken of us. He accused me of having an affair, cheating on his daughter. I denied it, of course, and I told him we were just friends. He promised me Laney would never know about you, and he also assured me that your husband would be given a job opportunity of a lifetime, far away from Savannah."

Charli could not believe what she was hearing. It was inconceivable. Grayson was used as a pawn in some game that Jack's father-in-law played? And played well. Their lives had changed for the better. Liam was making progress. Her marriage to Grayson was strong. All of that had come as a price though. She and Jack were separated by distance, and their friendship had been lost to them.

"Grayson can never know that," Charli finally spoke.

"Neither can Laney."

"We act as if your intrusive father-in-law was right and we do have something to hide," Charli stated. Maybe she was finally ready to talk about it with Jack.

"That's the worst part of this," Jack began, "because there is something between us. For the most part, we've left it unspoken, untouched. But it's as if it's so powerful and entirely above us. Every time we are together, there's an undeniable connection. I know you feel it, too."

"Why speak of it?" Charli asked adamantly. "Why acknowledge something that can't be? We are connected, and our souls speak to each other in a way that both fascinates and freaks me out."

"We need to face it. It will bring us closure. I followed you here today to say goodbye. You have been a gift to me. You arrived in my life at a time when I was giving up hope on my marriage and my potential career. I was coasting through each day without a purpose. I was as lost as Laney in some ways. You were like a compass. I felt like you guided me back on track. You also live with hardship, but the way you power through it inspires me and I felt encouraged to do the same. I needed you. I thought about you. I dreamt about you." Jack left out fantasized. It was inappropriate to say, but little did he know that Charli understood.

"I could in turn say all of the same things to you," Charli admitted. "I felt such guilt, but you became like an obsession for me. I think though, I finally see what we are supposed to take away from this."

Jack's expression pretty much said, *enlighten me, please,* as he waited for Charli to continue.

"It wasn't each other who we desired. It was what we took away from each other each time we released our frustrations and shared our troubles. What we held so tightly to was something the both of us were willing to give each other — a mutual understanding for the things that were constantly weighing us down, the encouragement to put one foot in front of the other and carry on. And love." Charli stopped talking, and the rate of Jack's heartbeat tripled. "By love, I mean the feelings we have for our spouses and now our children. That love became obligatory because we wanted it to. Those people are essential to our existence. Not us, not the two of us to each other. We can live and be happy without actually being in each other's lives. But, it's because we did cross paths and connect that we are now fully able to do that. Am I making any sense at all?" Charli asked him, after so many thoughts had unraveled in her mind for the very first time since she met Jack Horton.

Jack chuckled a little. "You are making the most perfect sense, and I finally feel like this wasn't wrong."

"If you would not have chased me down, and come here today, we may never have reached this point of understanding. It's peace, Jack. There's no other way to describe it. And it feels utterly amazing." Charli laughed. And there was such freedom in her laughter. She wanted to embrace that feeling —and Jack— but she did not.

OBLIGATED

"No one would ever understand this. Even if they overheard our words, it would be perceived as crazy," Jack stated what he believed was a matter of fact. This was both pure and simple, as well as tainted and complex. The abundance of emotions between them was something that anyone on the outside would be incapable to comprehend.

"Even if it was crazy," Charli said, referring to what happened to them, and how they were temporarily brought together, "I will never give up what I've gained from knowing you. I am going to carry the wisdom of your influence — and your spirit — with me for the rest of my life."

Charli felt the tears welling up in her eyes as she recognized the same in Jack's. He stood, Converse on the concrete now, and turned to her. "Close your eyes," he said, and she did, as more tears came and rolled off her cheeks. "Imagine me to hold your hand out of gratitude. Imagine me to pull you close to my chest so you can hear my heart beating with love. Imagine me to kiss your lips for no other reason than I am now at a loss for words."

Jack was crying now, too, as Charli opened her eyes. "Go on," he told her through tears. "Catch your flight back to your family." At first, she made no effort to move. And then he spoke to her one more time. "Goodbye, Charli with an I."

Charli choked on a sob. "And you… you go home to those beautiful girls in your life. Just know that each time I see your name up in lights, I'll burst at the seams with pride."

He didn't reach for her, nor she for him. There was no final touch, or embrace. Charli just turned to walk away and Jack remained standing just where he was all along. And, from a distance, a mere few rows of cars away, Laney sat behind the wheel of her minivan.

EPILOGUE, PART 1

When Liam was four and a half years old, a developmental pediatrician officially diagnosed him with Autism. It wasn't the worst thing in the world. It was hardly unexpected. Because it was, in fact, a long time coming. The reality hadn't left Charli and her ever-skeptical husband devastated. This label would open doors for more help that Liam would need as he matured. But it still hurt all the same.

Charli felt as if time was racing by while so many milestones had been passed over. She had a bazillion things on her mind at the doctor's office that day, but she spoke of none. Time could go right on ahead. She would wait — on the floor with her son while he reacted with tears or aggression — or alongside of him in the sand while the ocean waves washed over his contented body and mind. She was forever his mother. She was capable to wait for her son to be ready. And if that day never came, Charli would at least know she tried. With raw and real and fragile feelings, she tried.

Through dashed dreams and a lonely path less traveled, Charli would hang on. Among the odd and rigidity behavior, she wouldn't struggle to define it. She would just accept it. The moment she stopped trying to manage the things beyond her control was the defining moment of her journey with her son.

Charli prepared a picnic lunch with sandwiches and fresh fruit and a pitcher of iced tea. Grayson was coming home for a lunch that they planned to share on the beach today. They allocated more time for each other these days, especially while Liam was in school. They had not yet found anyone special enough in West Palm Beach, outside of school, who they trusted to leave alone with Liam. That was yet another reason to miss Vera Faye in their lives. Charli waited a little while longer for Grayson to come home.

Grayson was in his office, trying to step out to meet his wife for lunch. His boss sat on the edge of his desk in her short skirt. Her long legs were crossed directly in front of him.

"When are you ever going to give in?" she asked him.

"With all due respect, I'm committed to my wife," Grayson chose his words carefully. This was not a woman to overstep. His job was on the line.

She sighed and stood up, smoothing her skirt with her hands. "You never should have kissed me because now I know what I'm missing." His boss was right. It was a mistake that never should have happened. It did though shortly after their move from Savannah, when he was working closely with his sexy new boss, late one night. Grayson momentarily lost sight of himself and what he stood for. He was a man who loved and respected his wife. Grayson was absolutely certain Charli would never understand the force of attraction that could happen outside of a marriage. Or the guilt and shame that could come of it. Even if it was meaningless. Grayson vowed to never let it happen again. He had a wife and son, and a brand new baby on the way. Nothing was going to jeopardize that.

EPILOGUE, PART 2

Jack sometimes still rehashed that day in his mind. Charli was gone. He had watched her plane take off on the runway from the hood of his pickup. Afterward, he went straight home. His heart wasn't heavy. There was no confusion. His spirit had felt renewed. But he was crushed the moment he walked into the door.

The blinds were drawn in the living room in the middle of the day. Jack noticed the darkness as soon as he walked in. Laney's wheelchair was empty and parked near the end of the sofa where she sat oddly silent. She had a glass of wine filled to the rim on the end table beside her.

"Laney? What's going on?" Jack had charged right into the living room without stopping to remove his shoes. His first thought was panicked. *Had something gone wrong? Was Sabry safe?* His wife read his mind.

"The baby is fine. I asked Ashleigh, the neighbor girl to watch her for a little while." Ashleigh was a sophomore in college, studying to become a nurse. Laney knew her parents very well and trusted the entire family. Because Laney had unwavering confidence in Ashleigh, Jack did too. He still, however, could not relax. *Why would their baby have to not be at home? Had Laney needed a break?* Her glass was full and appeared to be untouched, but nonetheless she had the intention to drink alone in the middle of the day. "Was she your lover, Jack?"

Those words froze in the room as she spoke them. "I'm sorry, what?" *Jack really didn't have to ask her to repeat that, did he? He was still reeling from the shock of the realization that Laney knew. She knew he was with Charli. Her father must have been aware again — and followed them.*

"I drove to the store with the baby in tow." By *the store*, she meant JACK. "It was our first outing, other than going to the pediatrician for checkups. We wanted to surprise you for lunch. I parked alongside of the road just as you were coming out of the store and hurrying to your truck. I assumed you had an errand, or maybe you were headed home. I know you miss our baby girl sometimes."

"You followed me to the airport." Jack saved her the trouble of having to say it. "I can explain, Lane." *But could he? He may be able to tell the facts of the story, but would his wife ever truly understand or believe his explanation?*

"I want to hear what you have to say," Laney stated. Her brown eyes were icy, as the rest of her facial expression was equally as cold. "I need to know why you were visibly upset, talking to that woman in the airport parking lot. Body language says a lot, Jack. Even when you cannot hear what two people are saying to each other, the mannerisms, the expressions, and especially the tears, can tell so much of the story." Laney did notice they had never touched. Not once. She held onto that detail with absolutely everything she had. That would matter as she determined if their future would be together. Unless the touching… the kissing… and so much more had already happened in some sort of affair that finally ended near the runway.

"Her name is Charli," Jack began. "I met her over a year ago when my store was still empty and I used to sit near the window at my desk and design. There's a bus stop catty-cornered from the store. One day I watched this woman struggle to put a defiant child on a little school bus. And then when the bus pulled away, I witnessed her step off the curb and almost get hit by a car." Jack was starting at the very beginning. Yes, he was going to use the special needs or handicap card, but it wasn't to seek pity. It was to prove a point. *He and Charli connected over their hardships.* Laney's first thought was that Jack had never shared that story with her. Seeing someone almost get struck by a car was surely something to mention at the end of the day.

"The car sped off, and Charli had fallen back onto the curb. She was unhurt, but I didn't know that until I ran across the street to her rescue. She assured me she was fine, and we spoke for a few minutes. She asked where I came from so fast, I mentioned my empty store. I asked if that was her child she had put on the bus, and she told me her son had special needs." Laney felt her heart sink a little. Having a baby of her own now meant that she naturally sympathized, she was deeply affected by the mere thought of *something being wrong* with Sabry. "I sort of found a common ground with Charli at that initial meeting. My life changed right along with yours when you became confined to that chair, Lane." She continued to listen to him, while she also maintained the possibility in her mind that Jack had slept with another woman.

"Charli used to live in the apartment building near the store, the one where Vera lived. I just found out recently that they were neighbors and friends." Laney realized Charli was the woman Jack had spoken of, the customer in his store who had come back to town to take care of Vera during her last days. That explained the flight out of Savannah International. "I occasionally saw Charli at the coffeehouse. We would catch up on each other's lives, here and there. There was never an affair, Laney." Laney felt herself sigh a little. For sure, it was relief. "There was an attraction though." And now, just like that, her heart sunk. "It wasn't about desire. It wasn't about 'I have to have this woman.' It was her mind, her wisdom, her strength. Lane, I was drawn to learning how to cope with living a life not so normal. We got each other. She was obligated to her husband and son, as I was to you. And I don't mean it in the way that it sounds. I never felt forced or required to be with you. I wanted to be. You are the only woman I have ever kissed, ever touched and made love to." Jack watched a tear trickle down Laney's face and she never made any attempt to wipe it away. She remained motionless.

"Charli moved away with her husband and son more than a year ago. They struggled to make ends meet here in Savannah, and her husband received a job offer which made moving far away worthwhile. It wasn't fate or something that just happened to be in any sort of way though. It was the doing of your father."

"My father? What does he have to do with any of this?"

"He saw me a time or two in public places, speaking to Charli. He assumed the worst of me. He had someone take pictures of us talking. He confronted me, and I told him the truth as I'm telling you now, but in any case the all-powerful Richard Allison had to do more. He was the reason Charli's husband was offered a banking job for serious money."

"So he lied to me, too," Laney stated as a matter of fact.

"That's just it, Lane. There was nothing to lie about. Yes, I kept the fact from you that Charli and I were friends, but I didn't quite know how to tell you that I felt isolated in this house when I could not reach you anymore. I needed to face my feelings, too. And that's what Charli and I were able to do for each other. And today, at the airport, along the runway, we broke down the facts of what had really been going on. It was both uncomfortable and freeing. But, if you were watching us, you had to know our relationship was never physical."

"Do you love her, Jack?"

"I love what she did for me. I love how she indirectly opened my eyes to life's reality. And that is, sometimes we must alter our expectations in order to find happiness and contentment." Jack had no idea those words of wisdom had come from Vera Faye. Her spirit most certainly lived on in the lives of those she touched. "But do I love her? Have I ever been in love with her? No. I love you. You, Laney! I love that baby girl who's across the street right now and I want her back here in my arms and in yours. We all belong together. We are a family. Nothing matters more to me."

※

Laney was born and raised an Allison. The name was prominent and strong, her father had instilled that in her. After her mother died, her father raised her alone. He gave her everything. Spoiled her. She had all of the latest, priciest clothing styles, and a brand new hard-top jeep when she turned sixteen and earned her driver's license. But he also taught her how to be courageous and strong. After losing her mother, Laney learned to power through the pain and loss and the unfairness that life could launch at any given moment. Following her accident though, Laney had forgotten how to be that person. She allowed a wheelchair to define her. She lost herself for a very long time. And then she fought her way back to who she was and who she wanted to be again. She finally believed there had to be a reason she didn't die in that horrific car accident. That reason had turned out not to be her baby. It was Jack. It was the woman Laney wanted to be for him. In young Jack's eyes, Laney Allison had been the bravest. Through their years together, he learned from her, he desired her and wanted to be more like her. And then Laney changed. And Jack met a woman named Charli who gave him some of the things Laney once did. That truth was what awakened Laney the day Jack confessed his reason behind having a platonic relationship with another woman. She wanted to be that woman for him again.

It was near closing time at the store, and Laney was maneuvering her wheelchair between the clothing racks. They had rearranged and moved everything further apart to be better equipped in there for all people with handicaps. A new saleswoman they had recently hired told Laney she was leaving for the day. Laney locked the door behind her and turned off the OPEN light in the storefront window. And then she made her way to the back, to the only office in that building.

Jack was staring intently at the large computer screen in front of him. Laney glanced at the monitor before she spoke.

"It's closing time. I'm headed out to get our daughter. Ashleigh said she didn't have the best nap today, so we may be in for an overtired, fussy evening," Laney told her husband.

"That's my girl. She's just not interested in sleeping the day away. There's too much to do and see." Laney laughed as Jack spoke of their daughter as if she was much older than seven months.

"I'll see you at home soon. Want me to pick up something for dinner?" Jack offered.

Laney turned back to him, but she looked past him and over at the monitor on his computer again. "Shorten the zipper. I know it's a half-zip, but no woman wants the zipper to end underneath her breasts. It rounds us out too much. It most definitely fattens us from the profile more than we want." The signature sportswear style on the screen was one of Jack's latest designs. It was of a lightweight, dry fit material. The intention was for women to wear it while running or working out in any aspect. It was fitted, sporty, and sexy.

"What did you just say?" Jack's eyes widened.

"It was just an observation," Laney had caught herself too, and she was grinning at him now. She was on her way back to being the whole person she used to be. She hadn't lost her gift. Among chaos and confusion, it was just pushed to the sidelines for awhile. But now just felt like the right time to get back into the game.

"Get over here and tell me more!" Jack was smiling wide as Laney came to him behind his desk. He reached for her hand, and he saw the modest diamond ring he put on her finger the day he vowed in the Cathedral of St. John the Baptist to love her lifelong. That church, the skyline of Savannah, with spires at the structure's highest point, symbolized for them — then and now — how together they saw no limits and would reach new heights in their love and life together.

ABOUT THE AUTHOR

This story, unlike any of the others I've written, triggered something raw, real, and fragile in me. So much so, that I wasn't sure I could finish writing after I started a fictional story that, in parts, mirrors my own life. The last time I wrote about my son's Autism, he was just a little guy and I still had bigger hopes and greater expectations. He's now a preteen at twelve years old. With him, I've had dashed dreams and I've been on that lonely, less traveled path. He still has the rigidity and odd behaviors that no one can explain. And I've dwelled on those bazillion things as time continues to race by him, hurdling over the many milestones he never reached. I think about how he's half of twenty-four years old, and if the next dozen years go by as speedy fast as the first, he very likely will still have the same struggles as a man as he does right now as just a boy. And then, I stop.

And I realize. I'm looking entirely too far ahead. I'm trying to manage things beyond my control. I'm really no different than any other mother, or father. I just want the absolute best for my child. I've also had to learn to alter my expectations quite a bit. My son is not the boy I thought I would have the day I held him for the very first time, and looked into his blue eyes. Little did I know then… he will not learn to read or write… drive a car… turn the tassel on his graduation cap… bring home his first love to meet his parents… and the list goes on, in my reeling mind. While there truly is no point to focusing on any of that, I have and I do. But, between the delicate balance of certainty and the unknown, I choose to live for the moment, believing I'm doing the best I possibly can for my son who's innocently counting on me. So instead of focusing on what my son will never do, I proudly recognize everything he already has accomplished and has brought into my world, his dad's world, and his big sister's world. Because of him — we appreciate the little things, we have more compassion than we know what to do with, we laugh harder, and we love deeper — because we know life changes in an instant and challenges can alter everything.

As I continue to write the stories that allow me to escape from reality (if only for a little while), I'm beyond grateful to have a following of readers who are not only unwavering and loyal, but encouraging and inspirational to me.

As always, thank you for reading!

love,

Lori Bell